# Zane PRESENTS

# SHOW STOPPAH

## Dear Reader:

Thanks for picking up a copy of *Show Stoppah* by Thomas Slater. I am very excited about this book that deals with the life-altering ramifications of abuse on females. Empowering females has always been my main platform so to see the subject matter tackled in both an engaging and informative way fills me with delight.

Kimpa and Isis are two young ladies, united by the fact that they both landed in the same shelter for abused women. Even though all of the women there have battle scars, theirs are on an entirely different level than being smacked around every now and then, or yelled at for not having dinner on the table on time. Kimpa fell in love with the Devil and Isis was kidnapped and forced into hell by his twin brother, Satan.

After deciding that enough is enough, in a single act of desperation, they grow determined to let the world know about their traumatic backgrounds. They resort to taking over the radio show of a male chauvinist pig, and then they spend the next six hours retelling their miseries. While their situations are extreme, on any given day there are hundreds of thousands of women across the globe, possibly millions, who are being subjected to various forms of abuse. *Show Stoppah* is a great example of how simple venting can increase one's self-esteem tremendously. Victims do not have to remain victims; sometimes they can become "sheros."

As always, thanks for supporting Thomas Slater and the other authors that I publish under Strebor Books International. We try our best to bring you the future in publishing today with cutting-edge, risk-taking titles that spark thought, conversation, and controversy.

If you would like to join my email list, please send a blank email to eroticanoir-subscribe@topica.com. You can also find me on Facebook, on Twitter at "PlanetZane" or join my online social network at www. PlanetZane.org. My personal email is Endeavors@aol.com and my personal web site is www.eroticanoir.com.

Blessings,

*Zane*

Zane
Publisher
Strebor Books International
www.simonandschuster.com/streborbooks

ZANE PRESENTS

# SHOW STOPPAH

## THOMAS SLATER

STREBOR BOOKS

NEW YORK LONDON TORONTO SYDNEY

F
SLA
AA

Strebor Books
P.O. Box 6505
Largo, MD 20792
http://www.streborbooks.com

© 2011 by Thomas Slater

ISBN 978-1-59309-339-6
ISBN 978-1-4516-0797-0 (ebook)
LCCN 2010940496

First Strebor Books trade paperback edition April 2011

Cover design: www.mariondesigns.com
Cover photograph: © Keith Saunders/Marion Designs

10  9  8  7  6  5  4  3  2  1

Manufactured in the United States of America

For information regarding special discounts for bulk purchases, please contact Simon & Schuster Special Sales at 1-866-506-1949 or business@simonandschuster.com

The Simon & Schuster Speakers Bureau can bring authors to your live event. For more information or to book an event, contact the Simon & Schuster Speakers Bureau at 1-866-248-3049 or visit our website at www.simonspeakers.com.

Lord, I just want to say...thank you!

To my siblings of course: I love you guys—Wayne, Gloria,
and Jermain Slater!

This book is dedicated to all those that have touched my life in one way
or another: the Slater family, Posey family, Hicks family, Montgomery
family, Boggs family, Ramsey family, Lee family, Smith family,
Richardson family, Jones family, Sims family, Scrues family, Patton
family, Claybone family, Rawlins family, Bush family, Watts family,
Brogdon family, Snipes family and Duncan family.

If I've forgotten anybody, remember: for what my mind failed to store,
my heart holds you for sure!

I will forever treasure the memories of my father, Hugh E. Slater, Sr.
and my brother Hugh E. Slater, Jr., affectionately known as "June."
And if I can, I'd like to grab just a moment of silence for my cousin,
Roy Bradham. I miss you, man! R.I.P.!

# ACKNOWLEDGMENTS

There once was an Angel who was chosen for an assignment on earth. She said, *yes*, and took the job without further words. This angel in flesh was born and grew up to be a powerful woman with words of fire and infectious kindness. She walked softly and God had her back. Love was her second name and sacrifice, her native tongue. She labored tirelessly and effortlessly in the vineyard knowing one day she would get to return home, just to hear God's words of praise: "Job well done my good and faithful servant." And then it happened; she was called home to her reward. This angel I know well…she was Mary Slater—none other than… my mother.

I LOVE YOU, MA!

"This fucking food is disgusting, girl," Isis commented, pointing to her plate with her fork. "Beggars can't be choosers, but damn, is this supposed to be lasagna?"

Isis' body was thin, wiry, with vanilla-colored skin impressively stretched over ridges of lean muscle tissue. She was average height but nicely portioned, with shoulder-length hair.

Kimpa cracked a sheepish grin. Kimpa Peoples was the closest thing to physical perfection that one could reach. Some said she favored the platinum, Grammy Award-winning pop-superstar, Rihanna. She possessed all the voluptuous assets men desired, including high cheekbones, a slender face accented by long, flowing black hair and a magnificent swell in the bosom department. But her best features included: long, flawless legs, adorable bedroom eyes, and a tiny waistline.

"The food at this shelter ain't supposed to taste great," Kimpa said, picking up a cold, hard biscuit and banging it against the table, creating splintering breadcrumbs. "This is a shelter. The folks in here afraid that if they start serving that five-star gourmet shit, us po' folk ain't gonna take the initiative to go out in the world and gain our independence. I'd give anything right now for my bubble bath, aromatherapy, lobster, and champagne ritual."

"That sounds delicious, but expensive," Isis said.

Kimpa stared at her food. "It's a habit I picked up on Stan Larkin's dime."

"That your first trick, right? The lawyer guy?"

"He put me up at the Ritz-Carlton and I ordered room service until I puked. I'd chill out in a bubble bath, surrounded by scented candles, eating lobster and drinking champagne."

"Spoiled heifer," Isis said, teasing.

The two women laughed a little, easing the stress and tension in the air of the tiny, cramped enclosure passing for a cafeteria. The Woman's First Shelter transcended racial boundaries to help, heal, and provide support for women who'd been physically and mentally abused.

Kimpa and Isis sat at a table for two, eating in the presence of other women from different ethnic backgrounds, all bound tightly together by the universal bonds of heartache, pain, and suffering. "Pain doesn't recognize color," was the Woman's First motto, proudly displayed and beautifully painted in bright colors, across one of the walls of the corridor leading into the cafeteria.

"Kimpa, can you believe that broad over there?" Isis whispered, nodding her head at a dark-skinned woman wearing a weave pulled back into one long ponytail, sitting at a table in the corner by herself.

Kimpa turned her head. "Who you talking about?"

"Let everybody in here know we're gossiping, why don't you!" Isis chuckled. She discreetly nodded in the woman's direction again. "The sistah with the bad weave sitting in the corner."

"Yeah, ain't that rough? Her boyfriend was having threesomes with her and their ten-year-old daughter before he disappeared with the child. He left the sistah with nothing but tons of guilt and bad memories," Kimpa said, sipping on a glass of fruit punch.

"I hope the law catches up with his ass, cuts his nuts off, and makes him wear them around his neck." Isis frowned at the contents on her plate. "A reminder that a sickness like his can only be cured by castration."

"Amen to that, girl. Gimme some," Kimpa said, dapping Isis.

Isis thoroughly examined the cafeteria, taking in all the casualties who'd managed to break free from the painful grip of misogynist-masters and who'd been lucky enough not to have been numbered amongst those women who'd fallen to the bloody feet of a much more sinister circumstance.

"This shit's terrible, Kimpa."

"What, these hard biscuits?"

"Get serious. I'm talking about all these women who've been sent here because of ungrateful-ass, selfish muthafuckin' men. Well, with the exception of the Latina lesbian broad over there, Resa. Kimp, how long have we been shacked up at this shelter?"

"About six months."

"Six months too long. I mean, all we ever do is sit around in a group, cackling about how badly we were treated. It's the same routine every single fuckin' day. And I'm about fed up to my nipples with it. Nothing's getting resolved; the bastards that we complain about are still walking around out there in the street. The way some of these women have been mistreated, those bastards should've been locked away."

"I agree with you one hundred percent. They say it's a man's world."

Isis rolled her eyes at her plate before covering it with a napkin. "We're here eating garbage. Them niggas out there who are responsible for us ending up in here, what do you think they dining on?" She pushed her plate away. "It sure ain't generic lasagna."

"What can we do about it?" Kimpa asked. "We're two women among many who've been used up and thrown away like trash, left in places like this to die of humiliation."

"Granted, some of these sistahs in this place can spin some tales, but nobody's stories in here compare to yours and mine.

Not that I'm trying to compare heartache and pain, but we've been through the storm. That's why I believe meeting you at this shelter was fate. Do you see the cynical looks on these heifers' faces when we recount the hell we've walked through? They look at us like we should be writing screenplays or some shit."

"Isis, sis, no disrespect, but sometimes I even find our stories hard to believe. And I lived the nightmare. Had my baby took…" Kimpa's voice flat-lined into soft sobs.

Isis handed her some napkins. "See, sis, that's what I'm talking about right there," Isis said, tenderly caressing Kimpa's free hand. "We got to start snatching collars to let these men know we can get grimy, too. That bastard of yours got away with taking your baby. Shit, at least you know where your baby is. I don't have a clue where in the land-down-under that yellow nigga of mine got off to with my child. But I'll tell you one thing; there are a whole lot of women in this country who need to hear our stories, girl."

An older lady, one of the servers, walked into the cafeteria dressed in a white apron, hairnet, and black-framed bifocals, carrying a portable radio. "They've been taking donations on the radio all day to buy shoes for needy children!" the lady yelled out to another coworker behind the serving counter. "Before I come in here, I took out my credit card and pledged two hundred dollars. Yes, I did."

"Well, Brenda, sit that radio on the empty table right there, turn the damn thing on, and get to work!" the coworker screamed back. Brenda switched on the radio.

"Hey, Detroit, it's five o'clock and you're on the dial with 95.5 FM radio, with everybody's favorite morning eye-opening shock-jock, Mindspeak the Truth," the very distinguishable, electrifying voice boomed from the speaker of the portable stereo system.

"It's rush hour and Mindspeak will be with you for your evening commute. Yours truly has been pulling double duty, baby, since six this morning; my normal work hours. But our Shoes for Kids Campaign telethon is underway and we'll be jumping off all day long, and since this is a worthy cause, I'll personally be on the dial as long as it takes to champion this cause. We're trying to put shoes on shorties, man, so we need you to go into your wallets and make a monetary contribution, or you can purchase a pair of shoes and send them to 1000 Fourth Street, Suite 120, Detroit, MI 48233."

"I hate his undercover, woman-bashing ass," Isis said with enough sauce in her voice to earn a few glares.

"I don't know what you're talking about, but people are staring," Kimpa said.

"I'm five past giving a damn. How can you women listen to this chauvinist dog? And in a shelter for abused women, for Christ's sake," Isis ranted.

"Mindspeak has done some good things for the city," proclaimed a white woman with dirty blonde hair.

"I don't give a damn," Isis retorted. "Have ya'll ever listened to the man's topics? They're inflammatory. He always goes out of his way to make the man look like the victim."

"Sometimes they are," added an inky-black lady with an ugly scar on the left side of her mug.

"It's clear that group discussions aren't helping you, Barbara," Isis scolded. "Sweetie, you still think it was your fault that your boyfriend went off the deep end and tried to carve his initials in your face with a Rambo blade."

"That was pretty cold, Isis," Kimpa scolded her.

"Barbara, I'm sorry; didn't mean that crack. It's the pressure; that's all," Isis apologized.

Mindspeak spoke again from the radio. "Today's topic is women who kill their abusive lovers. If found guilty in a court of law, should their actions warrant them life in prison?" Mindspeak paused. "This should be a touchy topic. Men, I need to hear from you. Sistas, I'm gonna hear from the brothers the first half of the hour, but don't get 'em in a bunch because the second half belong to you. Hit me up on the hitter; call me at 222-SPEAK."

"You see what I mean?" Isis said, the fire in her eyes present for all to see.

"Look at how the switchboard is lighting up," Mindspeak boasted. "Caller, are you there? State your name."

"Yeah, Mindspeak, baby boy, this is Lil' Mike and yo' show is da bomb, big b-a-b-y. I want to congratulate you on the success of yo' show going national and thangs," the caller said in a deep voice. "But to answer yo' little question and thangs, hell yeah, them broads should receive life for killin' kangs. They were put on this earth to serve our purpose, made from our ribs, but somehow they got it twisted that they can talk back and not get smacked up."

"Very interesting perspective, caller, but we're going to take another. Hi, caller, what's your name?"

"This is Robert Macky at the Chrysler plant on the North side. And yeah, give them rats life. Likes I tells 'em on the job, play-boy, equality is equality. You want to work like a man, be pre-pared to suffer a man's pain. They should be at home barefoots, pregnant, and cookin' a $#!*%@!"—the censor kicked in—"dinner anyway."

"You hear them, ladies. Though their way of thinking might be straight from the Stone Age, they make a serious point," Mindspeak said. "What's good for the goose is always good for the gander. Listen, family, tomorrow's the last day before I go on vacation.

I'm gonna leave out of here with a banging show. Tune in here tomorrow for the big celebration. "

Isis went off. "That's the kind of fucked-up thinking that's put a lot of us in this shelter today. Fuckin' Mindspit." Isis was trying to be respectful of the older women serving the food, but she couldn't help herself. Her temper was boiling, nostrils flaring like the hood of a dangerous cobra.

"You mean Mindspeak," Kimpa said.

"Yeah, whatever. His show is national, right?" Isis whispered.

"What are you getting at?"

"Just answer the question."

"Yeah. Why?"

"I just found the answer to our problem."

With a worried expression on her grill, Kimpa was afraid to ask, "What you thinking about doing?"

"What better platform to assist us in getting our stories out to all the battered women to inspire unity? To stand up and protect themselves from what happened to us?"

"Isis, where are you going with this?"

"It's collar-snatching time. We gonna hijack Mindbender's show. It's the perfect way to strike a blow for the female cause. Show all these macho assholes that women are far from inferior. What a great way to emasculate the so-called masters of control, by putting Mindblender's misogynist ass in his place."

"Isis, what the hell are you talking about?" Kimpa asked in a voice, dripping concern.

"Getting a few pistols, laying in waiting for old Mindscratcher to roll up in the parking lot tomorrow morning, taking 'im hostage and forcing our way into the building. It's perfect! And while we hold the guns on Mindsucka, we can use the chump's national radio show to tell our stories, girl."

"What you're asking me to do is insane. Have you even factored the police into this little show-stopping equation of yours? And guns? I don't like guns."

Isis was intensely aware that Kimpa was worried. Hell, she was also a little apprehensive. She'd been so juiced up with adrenaline and rebellion, Isis hadn't factored in that they'd actually be running afoul of the law. The one thing that her ordeal had taught her was to grab the bull by the balls and squeeze tight.

"Listen, Kimpa, I can't promise you anything but a chance to take the power back from the sonofabitch who took your baby, and to take back your self-respect. A woman without it might as well be dead. You with me?"

Kimpa didn't even have to think hard. "Yeah. We sistahs for life. Let's do it."

"Okay, girl," Isis said, squeezing Kimpa's hands. "Mindsnitch is ours tomorrow morning, right before he goes on air. We'll be tuning in, alright. I promise you, he won't be celebrating after tomorrow's show."

A pain hit Kimpa in the stomach like she'd been kicked by a mule. It started in her stomach, with the aftershock registering in this unholy pain-face she was now wearing.

Isis grabbed Kimpa's hand. "Kimpa, you alright?"

Kimpa was holding her stomach. "The Old Lady's here."

"Oh, girl, your cramps bad?"

"Bad enough. Back when I was with Brody, I used to eat muscle relaxants like Skittles when she came to town. It was the only thing that took them away."

Isis examined the women in the cafeteria.

"I don't think you'll get muscle relaxants around here, but they might have some Midol."

"Isis," Kimpa whispered, "this is a bad sign. I don't think we should take down Mindspeak. I won't be of any use to you. My first two days are heavy and painful. I can't do anything but lay up."

"Look, Kimpa. You won't have to do much. We need to do this tomorrow. You heard Mindspender; he's going on vacation. I understand about your situation, but this can't wait. Trust me, it won't take long."

Kimpa submissively bowed her head, tears sliding down her cheeks effortlessly. She was confused and tired, wanting this chapter of her life closed. There was no running from the past. If anything, her life experiences had taught her to step on the past in order to walk to the future. This thing was going down regardless of the Old Lady's painful protest.

I yawned and stretched, covering my mouth, trying to conceal the fact that I was seriously having second thoughts. I was bloated and feeling yucky.

"Isis, there has to be another way. Let's go back to the shelter and think about this. Please, girl, we don't need this trouble—I don't want to go to jail. I still want a family. I can still salvage this life, I—"

"Kimpa, if you don't stand up for yourself, mothafuckas like Brody gonna run over you wherever you go."

"Isis, it's six in the morning and he's not here. We should take that as a sign and leave. Maybe God has—"

"I don't want to hear about Him because *He* wasn't there when I was gettin' my ass kicked."

Through the haze of my teary eyes, I saw a chance at humor. "Why's your gun bigger than mine?" I asked, sniffling and examining the small pistol she'd given me back at the shelter.

Isis eyed me with concern. She dropped her weapon in her lap, leaning over and hugging me. I couldn't help the tears that effort-lessly slid down, exposing the fact that I was a life giver and not a taker.

"Kimpa, it's gonna be okay. I got you. I promise you that I'm not gonna let anything happen to you in there." For a moment we were gently locked inside the consoling embrace of reassurance, looking like and pretending to be cold-blooded desperados. Well, I wasn't, but Isis was a different glass of water. There were no feelings. Her ordeal had robbed her of one of God's most pre-cious gifts. Isis was all woman, but her terrifying experiences had left her scarred and numb to compassion. Although we'd both had hard stories, hers was a little bit harsher. I couldn't blame her. All the death she'd witnessed had given her the ability to resist rational thinking.

"Kimpa." Isis straightened herself, wiping away the last of the tears on my cheeks. "We gonna be alright. Besides, beginners can't handle weaponry like this." She held up her big Desert Eagle, racking back the slide, smiling. "I'm the only one who's qualified to handle Roscoe."

We found the nerve to laugh a little, easing the tension inside the hooptie we'd stolen. In the early morning light, Isis' gun glistened like polished chrome.

"Promise me that nobody gets hurt, okay?" I asked of Isis, trying hard to gather the nerve to handle the pistol.

"I promise you, nobody gets hurt…but only if they're innocent."

We laughed again.

"Do I have to carry a gun? I don't like guns. They give me the willies." I grinned nervously. "Do you ever cry?" I wasn't trying to sound dainty, but I'd lost somebody whom I'd loved dearly to guns and I didn't want to go there.

"Yes, you have to go in there strapped. And no, I don't cry; I ran out of tears a long fuckin' time ago. All I got left is revenge," she responded.

We were two women with similar tales, sitting across the street from a nondescript building that housed the WBUD radio station. The station was home to "Mindspeak in the Morning," hosted by that male chauvinist idiot named Mindspeak. The show had started out locally, but had grown nationally within two years. I couldn't comprehend how his show could be ranked number one in the nation. His topics were always controversial, but cleverly devised to get under the skins of his female listeners.

We watched as an expensive SUV pulled into the parking lot. A burnt-black, ugly man stepped his short and stubby, fat-necked frame out.

My heart pumped ruthlessly against my chest. I had to dry my perspiration-soaked hands on the tattered, dirty-gray interior of the hooptie. I bowed my head to say a little prayer, but the brutal slamming of the passenger door snapped my head in the direction of the noise. Isis was out of the car, running full-tilt toward the man, who wasn't paying attention to his surroundings. The Starbucks coffee cup he was sipping from had his complete and undivided attention. Since it was so early in the morning, the streets were desolate. Isis caught and startled the man as he shrieked, throwing the coffee cup aside and shoving his arms in the air at the sight of Isis' Desert Eagle.

Truthfully, I was hesitant to bring the gun but I'd promised Isis. Half-heartedly, I was on Isis' heels, brandishing the nickel-plated 9mm and holding it like it had piss on the handle.

"What the fuck is this?" Mindspeak asked, trembling. He looked like he was about to piss his pants. His big bubble eyes were bugging out, darting from Isis to me. I had the misfortune of getting a close look at Mindspeak's face. The nigga was even uglier up close. I could see why he was always trying to get underneath women's skin. His kind of ugly couldn't get laid in a morgue filled with female corpses. I almost lost the sorry excuse for a breakfast the shelter had served.

"We're definitely not fans," I responded with my finger pressed against my lips.

Isis had the barrel of her pistol underneath his chin. "Keep cool, you little shit," she ordered.

"Please, don't shoot," he pleaded. "My wallet…my wallet has money in it. Take it, all you want—" His words were cut off as Isis dug the barrel of her weapon harshly into his throat.

"Shut the fuck up!" Isis commanded in a hushed voice, but loud enough to get his attention. "Don't get any ideas. My girl and I want a little time on the air."

"We better hurry up and get inside before somebody sees this scene and calls the police," I warned, trying hard to cover any signs of being a nervous wreck. I tilted my head toward the security guard, who looked to be nodding off behind a desk in the lobby. I could see him through a medium-sized window in the door but he couldn't see us.

"Once he buzzes us in," I said, "if he asks, we're with you."

"Anything. Just don't shoot. I have kids," he begged.

Isis cocked the hammer back on her weapon. "If you don't, you die. It's as simple as that." Isis' eyes were wild, giving her an unhinged look that backed up her threat. But just as I thought she was gonna go back on her promise, she winked at me behind Mindspeak's back, urging me to play along.

Mindspeak stepped up to the door with us in tow, sweating profusely.

Isis told Mindspeak, "I'm gonna put my gun outta sight, but don't get cute. Bullets can go through the pocket of this sweater."

The door buzzed. Mindspeak grabbed it, walking through with us right on his heels.

"Good morning, Mr. Mindspeak," greeted the chubby-faced guard with a Frankenstein forehead. The dude wasn't tall but his large, shapely Afro made him look enormous. He curiously examined us, awaiting recognition.

Mindspeak smirked, looking back at both of us. I thought Isis was going to pull the trigger, blowing holes in him because of the long pause Mindspeak took. He glanced around the well-decorated lobby, his eyes resting on the headless marble sculpture of a black nude torso posed in the corner. I could see clearly through the dangerous game he was playing. The nigga was trying to sweat us. But the stern look that Isis gave him was enough to scare me. I could see Isis' pistol hand tense.

Mindspeak coughed into his hand, then cleared his throat. He smiled slyly. "Marcus, the ladies are with me. They're my guests on today's show."

Mindspeak examined our unkempt appearances. Both of us looked like we'd crawled from under a rock. The shelter didn't have an iron, so our clothes were seriously wrinkled.

Mindspeak chuckled.

Isis pulled her pistol.

"Fuck this. Get your ass up," she ordered, shoving the pistol into Frankenstein's grill. The brother looked like he was about to mess his pants. The terror inside his bloodshot eyes was absolutely priceless.

Isis spotted a closed door right next to the statue.

"What's behind the door?" she asked.

"A clos...closet," Frankenstein stuttered badly.

"The keys on your belt. They fit the lock?"

"Isis, please," I said. She looked like she was coming unglued.

I had to pull her back. I couldn't live knowing that I'd caused some innocent man's death.

"Kimpa, I got this. Chill." Isis looked back to the guard. "The keys, do they fit?"

"Yes. Please don't do anything stupid," Frankenstein said.

"Too late for that. Now open the closet." Isis raised her pistol.

"Isis, what are you about to do?" I asked, almost dropping my gun to the floor.

I was trying my best to keep Mindspeak in check without breaking into tears while Isis marched the guard to the closet. Once it was open, the guard stepped in.

Just before slamming the door in his face, Isis said, "Now, I'm gonna need you to follow your own advice. Unless you want to be shot through this door, don't do nothing stupid. Now stay the fuck quiet." She took the ring of keys from his belt. "Which one's for the main door?"

He pointed out the key. Isis slammed the door hard, locking it. Then she went over to the main door and locked it, turning to look at me.

"There! You happy?" Isis asked me, sarcastically.

"Marcus wasn't going to cause ya'll any problems," Mindspeak said. "That man's got a family."

"I suggest if he doesn't want a hole in the head problem, he should keep his mouth closed," Isis snapped. "You better be worrying about yourself."

So far we'd been lucky. Other than Mindspeak and Marcus, we hadn't encountered anybody.

Isis was back from the door. She pointed her weapon at Mindspeak. "Let's go, flyboy."

"What is this about?" Mindspeak asked.

"The studio." Isis ignored Mindspeak's question. "Where the hell is the studio?"

Mindspeak headed down the hallway with us in tow.

"Kimpa, you need to get yo' emotional ass together and keep the barrel of your pistol up," Isis whispered to me as she marched behind Mindspeak. We made our way down an anorexic-thin hallway.

This entire thing was wrong, but it was necessary. We had horrible stories to tell, stories that women would respond to and that we hoped would help give women the strength to get away from abusive male oppression. However unbelievable they were, the stories would inspire. Hell, I'd gone through my painful ordeal and I couldn't believe it. And the story that Isis had confided in me with when we'd first met at the shelter was even harder to believe than mine.

Nobody said anything as we made our way to a studio that was encased in transparent glass. A beautiful black woman with dazzling shoulder-length hair busied herself in a room adjoining the studio. The lady had her back turned to us as we stepped up to the glass.

"Who's the black Barbie?" I asked.

"My producer. She's the one who runs the show," Mindspeak informed us.

With her gun out, Isis wasted no time rushing into the room. She looked back toward us, gesturing with her head for me to bring him in.

"He dies if you don't do what I say!" Isis said to the lady. I reinforced the threat by aiming my pistol at the back of Mindspeak's head. "Listen, here's the deal. My girl and I need a little time on the show to let the nation in on how bad we've been screwed around by men like this pig," Isis said, nudging Mindspeak with the barrel.

"This is absurd!" Mindspeak spoke up. "Lots of people have problems, but they don't go around"—he looked from my gun to Isis'—"hijacking radio stations to get heard." Mindspeak was treading in dangerous waters. I could see Isis' facial expression mutate into pure rage. Then, just like that, the heifer smiled at me, showing me that she could control her anger.

"If you don't stop talking," Isis said, "I'm gonna shove this pistol up your ass. Now let's get to what we're down here to do." She looked at me. "You go in the studio first. I'll keep girlfriend here... What's your name?" Isis asked the woman, who was shaking worse than Don Knotts.

"Don-na," she said slowly, almost as if she were in a trance. Then she appeared to pull herself together. "My name is Donna," she said more confidently. She blinked rapidly, never taking her eyes off Isis' pistol.

"Me and Roscoe here," Isis held her pistol up, smiling, "we'll keep Donna company. Remember, keep that pistol on Mindbender."

"That's Mindspeak," he corrected before I walked him out the door.

In the studio next door, Mindspeak tried to reason with me.

"Hey, look, you seem like the logical one. Why don't you talk some sense into your friend before ya'll get yourselves into deep trouble? If you leave now, I'll forget about the whole thing. No police will be called. We'll simply call it a misunderstanding."

"For Christ's sake, listen to me, please," I said, the warning in my voice was clearer than the picture offered by a Blue-ray player. "I'm trying hard to keep my sistah from doing something she might regret. Please work with me on not pissing her off, okay?"

"If you care anything for your sister, you'd talk some sense into her."

I cringed as I felt a sudden pain in my lower back, hips, and inner thighs. Felt like a bus was running over my insides.

"You alright?" Mindspeak asked.

"Yes. I'm fine. Let's continue."

"Put the headphones on," he instructed. Then he stared into the room at Donna, who looked like she was counting down. Donna's long face still held a look of terror.

"If you guys reconsider, you can walk out the door and I won't even call the police, but—"

"Five, four, three, two, one."

He spoke his signature greeting. "You're on the dial with 95.5 F.M. radio, with everybody's favorite eye-opening, morning-time shock jock, Mindspeak the Truth. Today we have a pair of interesting sistahs in the house." He glanced down at my weapon. "Women with a serious purpose. America, these sistahs have something interesting to bring you, so give them your complete and undivided attention." He looked at me and smiled. "Ladies and gentlemen, boys and girls, I'd like to introduce our first guest."

My heart skipped a beat. I took a deep breath, trying to ease my anxiety, but still, a single tear fell down my cheek. "My name is Kimpa Peoples." I took another deep breath. "And I've been a victim of abuse. I've been physically abused, raped, and beaten within inches of my life, and to top it off, my no-good baby daddy was an expert at self-made abortions. I've been a victim multiple times." I couldn't help but notice Mindspeak cringing. "You see, my baby's father is Brody."

Mindspeak looked at me, the question in his eyes.

"Brody, the famous urban novelist, screenplay writer…million-aire," I said slowly, making sure that everybody recognized which Brody I was talking about. "The courts wouldn't listen to my story. And because Brody is worth millions of dollars, they awarded sole custody of my baby to his foul ass."

"Mindspeak in the Morning" was one of Brody's favorite morning shows, and I knew the bastard was listening wherever he was, and cringing. "He used all his power and influence to take my baby, my clothes, my self-respect—and put my ass out on the street." I looked at Isis. She was nodding her approval. Even Mindspeak looked eager to hear my story.

I relaxed, powerfully and painfully summoning up the demons of the past, my eyes leaking tears like maintenance-neglected faucets.

A ll I ever wanted in this miserable life was to be happy. I was raised in a Christian household by a strong, black, Southern woman who was strong in her commitment to the Lord. Poppa died when I was eight, leaving my mother with the heavy burden of raising her only child in the fast-paced, mean, and ugly city streets of Detroit.

My momma was a proud disciplinarian who was dedicated to ensuring the proper upbringing of her little girl. She would never let anything or anyone get in the way of the promise she'd made to Poppa on his deathbed: to take care of his little girl and never let anything negative befall her. Momma cried a lot out of loneliness. Although she wanted to date again, the idea of bringing another man into our household petrified her.

In the short time that my parents had together, I'd watched and learned a lot about being a wife and mother. My momma instilled old-fashioned values in me that she hoped would come into play when I got married and had kids. But she would leave her work unfinished. Momma was killed on a city bus. It was reported to me that two men started arguing about a seat and one man produced a handgun. Momma's life had been taken away, torn from me because some fool thought that he was being disrespected.

I was sixteen with no place to go and no relatives to turn to.

Broke and hungry, I lived on the streets, until I met a baby-faced man named Brody Ellis. Brody was homeless also. We met in a shelter and I was instantly beguiled by his talk of goals and dreams. Boyfriend was an aspiring urban writer with visions of bestselling material. I was impressed. The knowledge of literature this man possessed! Although I hadn't finished high school, I'd studied Shakespeare, Richard Wright, Herman Melville, and a few others. I couldn't believe that this man with all these great visions was homeless.

The more I kept Brody's company, the more he reminded me of Poppa, another strong black man who'd deserved a chance in this cruel world. And even though I was charmed by his hopes and dreams, the uncut truth of our union was that I needed this man. Being homeless, two was always better than one. The streets were dangerous for single homeless women and the likelihood of survival was cut in half without somebody watching your back. A sistah had to do what a sistah had to do.

"Baby," Brody said, "I want to be your friend, your lover, your husband, and your father. I want to take care of you." He glanced around the rinky-dink, third-rate motel room he'd hustled up to hold us a couple days while I recovered from the flu.

"You hungry, baby? I talked the man up front into supplying us with a hotplate. Got some chicken noodle soup over there on the table." We lay spooning underneath the covers on a bed that'd probably seen more action than a Rambo movie.

I nodded my head yes, hating it when Brody got up, leaving the cold draft of chilly air in his place. He was completely bare. He might not have been a sex symbol but he was my white knight, saving me from the harshness of a bad nightmare. In his mid-twenties, standing six-feet even, Brody was slender, the only fat thing on him being his stomach. His skin was the color of the finest ebony; chocolate to perfection. Even though he kinda looked like Forest Whitaker with bony legs, my baby was gifted where it counted.

It was cold out, unusually so for the month of October, but our room pulsated with the warmth of love.

"Baby," Brody said, warming up the soup, "I'm gonna take care of you. Ain't no flu bug gonna get the best of my honey. Baby, can you remember the look on the doctor's face last night after I rushed you to emergency in the cab? Like we had no right to be there because we didn't have any insurance. But they had to treat you anyway. You scared the hell outta me, running that high fever. Thought you weren't gonna make it."

"Fooled you. God looks after His own," I said, closing my eyes, still drained by our all-night stay in the E.R. I didn't see a doctor until the early hours of the morning. The things the homeless have to go through.

Brody poured the soup into a Styrofoam bowl. "Sit up," he instructed, his sexy, thick lips blowing on the soup to cool it. He took the plastic spoon and dipped it in, carefully bringing the soup to my mouth. I tasted it, making a face.

"Too hot?" He blew again. "It's hard to hustle up money these days. It was wrong but I had to get your medicine by ripping aluminum siding off a vacant house, filling up the buggy, and pushing the thing miles to the scrap yard to sell it for money. But you're worth butchering my bunions for, Pumpkin."

Brody wasn't slick. Whenever he started using the *Pumpkin* line, it usually meant he was trying to soften me up. And I realized what he was buttering me up for. I could practically smell his intentions. He wanted to have the *talk*. I'd been down that road with him dozens of times, with him trying to convince me to use my assets in funding his passion to become a bestselling author so that we could get off the streets and move on up like George and Weezy. And it always ended with his jaws tight. I wasn't that desperate yet. But I ate the extra attention up anyway, just melted, blushing like a schoolgirl receiving her first kiss. It felt good to be fussed over and treated like a queen. And even though the room wasn't the romantic palace I'd envisioned, being there with Brody, I felt like he was my big, strong protector. Nobody could harm me.

Brody fed me the last of the soup. "Pumpkin, it's time to take your medicine."

My baby's ass was tight and firm. I watched its movement as Brody walked over to retrieve my meds from the table. I'd been prescribed amoxicillin the size of horse pills, and cough syrup.

"Pumpkin," Brody sweetly said, "I'm not asking you to do nothing that I wouldn't."

"C'mon, baby, please, not this conversation again. I told you: I need some time to think things through."

He poured the liquid into the spoon. "Here's the airplane." He aimed the spoon at my mouth, laughing. "Open up the hangar."

I giggled, coughing, almost hacking up a lung. Brody was silly, yet he knew how to get what he wanted.

"Baby, I did the whole male escort thing for a while—"

"*Male escort?* Stop bullshitting me, and stop trying to underplay it. You want me to be a prostitute."

"—and plus I'll be watching you every moment."

"And what would that be saying about me? It would go against all my morals, everything that my mother taught me. I just can't."

Brody lay back down in the bed, taking me in his big, strong arms. "Haven't I taken care of you up to this point, Pumpkin?"

I slowly nodded.

"Pumpkin, God knows how hard it is down here for people like me and you. He's a God of patience and understanding, plus He's given us room for error. Sometimes He wants us to take two steps toward Him. Please, baby, it'll be for just a quick minute. All I need is money to get self-published—"

"What you mean, all *you* need is the money?" I asked with sauce in my voice.

Brody smiled, wearing the dumb look most men wear when they figure out they've swallowed enough foot.

"You know what I mean. *We* can get the manuscripts published—with this, *we* can get enough money to get *us* off these streets and into the literary world."

"Do you know what you're asking me? I thought I was all yours. How could you part your mouth to ask this of me?"

"Listen, I never had anything but my dreams. Even when my job packed up and left me unemployed with a serious crack problem, I fell into depression and the next thing I knew, I was on the streets—"

"But you're not the one having to fuck strangers and subject yourself to STDs, perverts, and crazy-ass fools, Brody."

"Kimpa, I got you. I kicked the crack pipe. We can do this, baby. Just like you, my mother passed away when I was a teenager. Never had a father. And Momma's boyfriend, the only father figure I had, used to beat the shit out of my mother and me. That fool used to get drunk and we became his own personal punching bags—"

I interrupted his rambling. "You're asking me to put my health in jeopardy—HIV, STDs, and a whole library of shit could kill me, or at least prevent me from getting pregnant."

"I'd never let anything happen to you on them streets."

I tenderly stroked his cheek. "You promise? Make me a coauthor on the book and the deal is done."

"Sure, Pumpkin. I love you. I promise. It won't be but a quick minute, business partner."

Brody randomly painted certain areas of my face with kisses, the forehead kiss being the most endearing. I stopped him from making lip connection. No need for both of us to be sick. He needed to stay healthy to take care of my needs. But Brody wouldn't take no for an answer. He continued his quest to show me his appreciation for my sacrifices by tunneling straight down, past my navel, and licking me like I was his favorite ice cream cone, verbalizing his thanks between passionate pecks, kisses, and licks. I was loving it, eating it up, as I spread my legs for him to lap at me and lavish me with praise.

I was "woman" and that word was stronger than any powerful accomplishments made by a man. I would enslave the power and make it work for me. I would build the empire of my dreams, even if I had to perform this one trick at a time. Over the years evolution pimped us girls out to be cerebral masters. Where men possessed physical capabilities, women were bred to be crafty, creative, and clever. We're often considered the weaker sex but that "weakness" is measured only in terms of physical strength, not guile.

And while Brody pleasured and praised, sucking me like I was a flesh-flavored lollipop, I was plotting and strategizing. I wanted off the streets, badly! Badly enough to use my body to get me a piece of the American dream. But I was clever enough to let him think that he'd come up with the plan. I was ashamed of myself for lying, but there was no room on my empty dinner table for the truth. Yeah, I'd gotten caught in a situation or two where I had to sell my body to put food on the table. I hadn't looked at it as prostitution. It was a necessary evil. This time it would be different. I wouldn't be alone. Besides, I needed the muscle. Brody would handle the fools that got crazy, like the last trick that I'd dealt with a month before I met Brody. The second john turned out to be a psychotic, twisted fuck that tried to choke me inside of his climactic moment. His crazy-ass was also the one responsible for me stopping the sale of my goods-for-food campaign. It was a promise that I'd made to myself until now. Brody would have my back—that I was sure of.

My plan was simple: we would go with Brody's plan for getting his manuscript out there, a minimum of two years at the least. Momma always taught me never to place all of my eggs in one basket. So, I would store my own money in a different location, in case Brody's plans failed. God and my mother would disapprove of me ditching my morals for life-changing money. But like I said before: I had to do what I had to do. Yes, I did love Brody, but I was more in love with what we could do for each other.

My first night on the street was memorable. After going on a perilous shoplifting spree, I had the wardrobe that was needed to put my plan in motion. My dream was of having a castle-sized home with artsy pictures hanging on the walls.

Brody tried to show me how to be sexy, but that was like a dog trying to show a horse how to bark. He didn't get it. Women were the owners and originators with a lifetime patent on sexy.

I had to admit: I was a little jittery—okay, I was mortified. I couldn't believe how far I had to stoop in order to reach for security.

One of Momma's jobs was on Woodward Avenue, housekeeping for this sleazy motel. Ironically, it was the same motel that I was standing in front of now. As a child, I used to go to work with Momma. I was fascinated by the wigs, long eyelashes, makeup, and five-inch heels worn by the sexy women who frequented the place. Sometimes I would get caught gawking at the women and men who came into the motel. Then Momma would snatch me up by the ear and tell me that I was looking at wicked, evil women of Babylon. She told me that if I stared long enough, Satan would see my curiosity, add me to his list of trashy heathen women, and I would be eternally doomed to a life of cruel pimps, heartache, and crotch-damning diseases. She would shake her finger in my face sternly and put me to work. I really hated to think this but I thank God that she was gone and didn't have to see her daughter's shame. I was now officially one of those women she'd despised, dismissing them as weak whores, wearing Satan's paint. But I didn't see myself as a whore; I was a businesswoman. Momma could say what she wanted: her little girl was on a mission for financial stability.

It was September 5th. The first week of the month had brought record-breaking cold temperatures. I tried hard to pull the short skirt that I was wearing down around my knees. As I walked into traffic, I drew a sea of stares from other working women and johns alike. I was the freshest young tender on the track. I strutted down the sidewalk, trying hard not to stumble in my stilettos. I couldn't see how in the hell the girls who stripped in the clubs danced around in these shoes. It took some getting used to, but I managed a seductive swagger, putting a little more twist in my hips to throw men into a horny-ass frenzy, not being able to open wallets fast enough to shower me with cash from their hard-earned paychecks. I had to admit, all the attention that I was receiving was flattering.

Brody took up his post across from an old burned-out supermarket. He'd promised that he would watch out for me and keep me safe from police and maniacs. The flaming red skirt hugged me like a glove, accentuating my every curve. I stepped right out into the ocean of humanity. Hearing the approving horns of passersby only added fuel to my strut.

"You bitch," I heard one of the older working girls say. The lady reminded me of my grandmother. Baby girl had on a cropped top that revealed an out-of-shape bag of a belly and a super-skin-tight miniskirt that left visible her pudgy legs stained by awful stretch marks. I paid her no mind as I stepped right up to the john who was about to select her but saw me and dissed the hell out of baby girl. Why drive an old, out-dated jalopy when you can grip the road in a super-sleek sports car. Outdoing her tired old ass had been my motivation for walking up to the Cadillac with the white man wearing shades inside, but I realized as I approached the car that I didn't have a clue what to do next.

I glanced over the roof of the car and locked eyes with Brody, hoping he would tell me that he had hit the lottery and I wouldn't have to perform such a degrading act. There was no such luck. He simply nodded his head. I swallowed hard. Sometimes the best-laid plan wasn't easy to carry out. And here I was, down to give it away for a hot meal and lodging.

Darkness was settling over the track. The man pulled down his shades and peered over them.

"Hi, sugar. You're looking real tasty tonight." He smiled brightly. He was an older gentleman.

I forced a smile and tried to speak but the words stalled in my throat.

"Easy, baby, I'm not a cop." He flashed a roll of cash. "I'm looking for a good time." I pegged him to be some kind of businessman. His navy blue suit, tie, and briefcase gave it away. The plain gold band on his finger told me that he wasn't satisfied with his wife. "C'mon, sugar, get in." He reached over and opened the car door.

My mind and heart were racing a mile a minute. My whole life flashed before my eyes. This time was clearly different from the first. Back then, I felt that God had chosen to overlook my little sin-for-cash venture. Hunger had played a tremendous part and

He understood my desperate situation. But this time I felt like I was simply using what I had to get what I wanted, and that decision had "eternal-burning Hell" written all across it. I was using my ass to fund an enterprise and that had me worried. Stepping into the car meant that I would be turning my back on everything that I was taught about good morals and strong values. Momma's chilling words came back to haunt me: *"eternally doomed to a life of cruel pimps, heartache, and crotch-damning diseases."*

He smiled hard. "Don't worry, sugar, I won't bite."

I tried to force my legs to move. It was as if my mother had control over them.

They became stubborn, like her. As I placed one foot inside the car, news clips of serial killers ran through my mind like so many gory Friday night slasher movies I'd watched. Over the years, I'd seen my share of serial killers being arrested on the news. I tried to size boyfriend up. But almost all older white men looked like serial killers to me.

I finally forced my other leg into the car. I'd done it. There was no fire and brimstone like Momma had preached. But Momma never told me that Satan drove a Cadillac.

We parked in an alley two blocks from the pickup spot. I'd led him right to the spot that Brody and I had agreed upon earlier. Since Brody didn't have a car, we'd both agreed that the spot would be within walking distance, so that Brody could watch my back.

I looked around nervously. The alley was dark and gloomy. With the exception of a few stray dogs, there wasn't a soul in sight. I scanned the alley to see if I could catch sight of Brody's head peeking around the corner. Nothing. I had mace in my bra, just in case.

"Relax, sugar, I only want some loving." He laughed and added, "What you people call 'hittin it.' Yeah, I want to hit it."

He leaned his head to one side, narrowed his eyes, and smiled brightly. I couldn't believe how perfect this man's teeth were. "Don't tell me this is your first time, sugar?"

"Y-y-yeah," I lied, not knowing why.

"Well, I can't believe I lucked up and got fresh meat; meat that hasn't been contaminated." He laughed again. "Sugar, what's your name?"

"Penny," I lied again.

"Such a pretty name. I know we're supposed to get down to it, but I find you attractive and very mysterious. How old are you?"

I hesitated for a moment, not wanting to tell him that I was seventeen. If I told this man that I was underage, would he put me out? I'd have to force myself to perform. But finding a way out of being homeless was all the inspiration that I needed. Either I'd learn to completely detach myself from my work or continue to stuff newspaper inside my clothes for insulation on those cold, park-bench-sleeping, wintery nights. I'd made my mind up and it was hard for me to go back now.

I paused a while to allow myself to remember the plan. How bad could this life be? It would only take a year or two to get up the money we needed to finance the first phase of the plan. I needed a solid Plan B, in case this one fell through or—God forbid—something happened to Brody. I had to have a way of supporting myself. Going back to the street wasn't an option.

"Penny, look here." He reached under his seat and came out with a bottle of wine. "This should put you in the mood. I mean, relax you more than you are. I don't usually tell working girls my name but you look like I can trust you. Besides, I don't want this to be our last business dealing." He extended a milky-white hand. "My name is Stan—Stan Clark."

I took the bottle. I meticulously studied the seal on the screw cap. It didn't appear to have been tampered with.

"Nice to meet you, Stan."

"Penny, this is none of my business but how did you come to be in this place? I mean, you're a beautiful girl."

"That's a long story. We don't want to get into that."

I opened the bottle and began to take small sips. I felt a heavy fog roll over me. We drank and talked for a few moments. Stan told me that he was a lawyer. He had a wife and three kids. He lived out in West Bloomfield. He told me about his steamy obsession with BET videos and his red-hot curiosity to fuck a black woman. Said that he had developed a hankerin' for dark skin and big asses. I also learned that Trixy was the name of the fat-stomached hooker that I'd cut out of a john. Stan had been flirting with the idea of having her as his first black piece. Trixy was supposed to have been his first romp through the jungle of black fever. Now here I was with him.

Drinking with a stranger was taboo, but I felt comfortable with him.

"P-P-Penny," Stan stuttered badly. "It's getting kinda late. I think we should be getting down to business. I know you have other customers." Stan was wasted.

He sluggishly opened the door of his car and slid into the back-seat. He wasn't that big of a man so the backseat of the Cadillac was accommodating. I was also dead drunk; so high that morality was hiding its eyes from the events to come. So numb that the image of Momma's ghostly pleading face in my mind looked funnier than a silly-ass Jim Carrey face. So numb that I didn't feel Stan's two-inch dick entering me. So numb that the tears that stained my face in the darkness didn't deter me from my mission. So numb that I didn't even remember straddling Stan and bouncing up and down, trying to take out all my anxieties on this poor, pitiful married man.

Stan was holding on to my shoulder-length hair, grabbing, pulling and tugging, yelling, then whispering Halle Berry's name. Granted, I didn't know what the hell I was doing but too much wine had me loose. The car rocked from side to side, looking like Stan's ride was fixed with hydraulics. Stan made sure that he was grabbing my ass, acting out his fantasy. He became extra excited when my well-shaped, brown-skinned ass bounced, jiggled, and collapsed into his hands.

I was giving him the ride of his life. But all I felt was pain, and not the pleasurable kind that I'd heard girls talking about. My soul ached as my promise to my mother became a thing of the past. I'd betrayed her so deeply that I wanted to ball up into a knot and die. I felt as though my body was used up and I'd have nothing to give my husband on my wedding day. Then again, my future husband was the one who had my ass out there in the first place.

I finished up the demeaning session. I didn't know it but I'd put something powerful on the white man. Like they say, once you go black, it's hard to go back.

My head felt like Dumbo was standing on it. I got myself together and was ready to leave when Stan grabbed my arm.

"Sugar, don't you want your money?" In my shame, I had almost forgotten. He handed me the cash. "And here's a little extra to get a hotel room and get off the streets. Sugar, it's too dangerous around here. Get someplace nice to stay."

I was speechless. Stan was the perfect gentleman. Not once had he tried to play me out. His eyes were warm and inviting. His arm shook as he extended the fist of hundreds. I took the money, already figuring out where to hide the extra.

I stepped out of the car into a gust of wind, reminding me that I'd forgotten my panties and that I'd lost my value. The wetness I felt between my legs made me feel cheap and undesirable. I walked up the dark alley. I could see the bright lights from Woodward Avenue ahead of me. I needed to pretend like I was an A-list actress, playing the part of a prostitute to handle reality.

I glanced up at the sky, hoping that the clouds had obscured God's view of the alley. My thoughts were interrupted, my mouth went dry and a coldness set into my body as I suddenly remembered the condoms Brody had given me were still in my purse. I silently cursed my stupidity. Where was my damn mind, drinking wine, the powerful crippler of sound judgment? I panicked. An unwanted pregnancy didn't rank up there with the worries of HIV and other STDs, but still, the possibility filled me with fear. The fuck. Nothing was gonna slow me down. I was committed to getting my ass off the streets.

A hand came from the darkness, touching my shoulder. I shrieked.

"Pumpkin," Brody said, tenderly caressing my shoulder. "You all right?"

I said nothing as I darted into the secure warmth of his arms.

"This is our first step to stardom. Pumpkin, you sacrificed a great deal here tonight, but it'll all pay off." He ran his hand along my forehead. "This might feel degrading to you, but you have to believe in me. You do believe in me, don't ya?"

I nodded wearily. But it wasn't Brody I was really doing this shit for. My body was my own. And even though he'd handle the money, in my opinion he was hitching a ride. Regardless of whether his shit took off or not, I was getting the hell off the street.

"I know what I'm doing. Trust me. Today, we live like rats. Tomorrow, we sign our name in the Hollywood Walk of Fame. Do you have the money?"

Without a word, I handed him some bills. I wanted him to shut up with the sales pitch. I was running through an obstacle course of emotions. I wanted to cry, then I felt rage, wanting to take my heel off and wear Brody out until I could no longer hear my conscience screaming at me, calling me a whore. I didn't feel like dealing with Brody right now. I didn't really have a reason for being angry with him after willingly giving of my body, other than that he was the closest person around.

"Good. This is the start of something. We'll get a motel room tonight and plan our future." Brody held the money up to the moonlit sky. He held on to the bills like he hadn't felt or touched money in years.

He tried to reach for my hand, but I brushed him away, not wanting to be touched. I wrapped my arms around myself, struggling with painful emotions, looking down at our shadows on the concrete as we walked up the alley. His strut was full of hopes, dreams, and ambitions. My strut was that of a wet coochie whore in training. I felt dirty. The dirt that no shower could clean away. My dirt stained the soul. It was the kind of dirt that needed to be cleansed by prayer.

Although I had the looks and the body, money came slowly. Brody was useless. He didn't know the first thing about hustling; neither did I for that matter. All Brody was good for was keeping other pimps off my back. To send a message that I was off limits, Brody had beaten this pimp named Pimpin' Prince bloody with a table leg. That was my first look at Brody's mean streak. It was real nasty. Since then, pimps had stayed away out of fear of Brody and his table leg.

The real money came when we allied with this beautiful older girl named Sensation. We met under very unusual circumstances. I was getting ready to jump in Trixy's old ass when three of her crew stepped to her back. It was about to get real ugly, four on one when Sensation came out of nowhere brandishing a pistol, temporarily squashing the beef. She took an interest in me and showed me the ropes. She taught me how to really chase that paper and took me to all the hot spots. She had high-end clientele, men with serious cash to spend. Ol' girl got me plugged in to some of her people. Girlfriend was dark chocolate and possessed an hourglass figure. Next to me, Sensation was the hottest thing on the track, and she had an attitude. She had the respect of every other girl and pimp on the block. Much like Brody, Sensation's pimp, Boss, was a beast, too. He didn't fear Brody but had much respect for how he beat the brakes off Pimpin' Prince for trying to push up on me.

Sensation and I grew close. She watched my back and I watched hers. I'd never had a big sister before and Sensation filled that spot, for which I was thankful.

All the morals that my mother had instilled in me were history. Money had become my God. Hustlin' was my religion. To make it in this game, I couldn't afford to have weaknesses. I had to change my identity completely. For now, Kimpa Peoples was lost, replaced by a broad with sharper instincts and an everlasting eye for business. Simply put, I said goodbye, for now, to Kimpa and welcomed my new name—Delicious. Sensation said it fit me.

"Delicious," Sensation schooled me, "always be on your guard. Over the last three months, a crew of niggahs been kidnappin' bitches. And not just any ho. They after the bitches clocking the dollars. Girls like you and me. So get yo'self a pistol."

*Great*, I thought. I didn't like pistols. My mother had lost her life to one and I'd vowed never to put my hands on one.

I hugged her. "Sensation, thank you for all your help."

In the game, it was easy to lose yourself if the money was right. Sensation warned me, telling me that if I had a game plan, to stick with it. Never stray.

The money had already gotten to my big sistah. Sensation had

had a year to go at Wayne State before she was due to graduate. She had delivered a beautiful baby boy and was due to get married after graduation. It would never happen. Sensation's drug-dealing fiancé was gunned down at a nightclub, leaving her with nothing but memories. She was devastated. She hit the streets to take care of her baby and pay for school. She'd been on the track ever since. But unlike her, I had a two-year hustle plan that I believed would lead me to fame and riches as a coauthor on Brody's book, or ditching his ass if the plan didn't go as promised. I would get a job, a life, and move as far away from the city as I could.

It had been exactly one month since I'd made my deal with the devil for a future dream of living the lifestyle of the rich and famous. Brody and I moved into a flat that was piss-poor, but it was a far cry better than the flea-bitten motel rooms we'd been staying in. We'd accumulated a nice nest egg. And I'd managed to squirrel away a nice piece of change working tricks on the side. It was resting in CD accounts, earning interest under the name Sosha Winter. Not all of it though—a girl had to have her emergency money.

Since Brody was good with figures, he had control of the money. Brody didn't trust banks so he hid the money somewhere in the flat. When I asked him to tell me where, in case of an emergency, he snapped at me.

"Mind your mothufuckin' business! It's on a need-to-know basis! And you don't need to know!"

"Nigga, you must've lost your mind! I laid down for that shit every night and you think you gonna hide it from me? You got it twisted!" I yelled back.

"You right, I apologize. It's just the stress of trying to write and deal with other things."

I wrote off Brody's bitter outburst as being due to stress. He'd been putting in killer hours working on his latest manuscript, the contents of which he wouldn't tell me. The only time I would see him was when it was time to collect my trap money—I guess that's what it was called. I still didn't have the lingo down.

Our flat had two bedrooms. Brody used one of them as his office. There he stayed, locked behind the door almost twenty-four hours a day. The only time he came out was to eat, shit, and collect money. It seemed that Brody stopped touching me when I started on the street, which was all right with me sometimes; my own workload left me exhausted both mentally and physically. We hadn't had sex in so long I couldn't even give an accurate date. And when we did, he'd complained about my weight gain, which I'd been noticing myself. At first I hadn't been concerned about it, but then I developed morning sickness. My missed period was another indicator that I was an expectant mother. If it wasn't Brody's child, I had a pretty good idea whose it was. Stan was a regular customer. He was the only one that I was having unsafe sex with. He'd told me that he'd had a vasectomy and that his tadpoles weren't swimming upstream anymore. I assumed it was safe to tell him that his operation had been a joke and that a lawsuit was imminent.

When Sensation drove me to the clinic, everything was verified. I was pregnant, and devastated. We drove around for hours. I was crying and Sensation was preaching.

"Four-fuckin'-weeks! Are you kiddin' me? You're four fuckin' weeks' pregnant! I can't believe you could be so stupid," Sensation yelled. "Never let a trick run up in you raw. I don't give a damn if he claimed he had his nuts cut off. That shit ain't gonna stop no damn AIDS."

"Stop yelling. I already feel bad." I had my head down as if the answer to my problem would appear on the floor mat of Sensation's car.

"You sure it's not Brody's?"

"He hasn't touched me since I started the trade."

"That don't mean a muthafuckin' thing."

"I know that it isn't his, Sensation."

Sensation parked the car and we walked into a Coney Island restaurant. My big sistah was silent all the way in. We ordered our food and sat down at a table that'd been poorly wiped down. Little salt particles still remained, and half of a French fry. Sensation lit up a cigarette. She harshly rolled her big bubble eyes at a couple of brothers who were staring lustfully in our direction.

"Delicious, I'm not trying to be your momma. But I *do* care about you." She blew smoke from her mouth and nose. "You said that you had plans for life after the track. How in the hell you gonna have a future if you catch HIV?"

I felt like a scolded Cosby kid. But it felt good. It felt good for another human to express concern about me.

"What do ya think Brody is gonna say?" Sensation asked concernedly. She knew Brody's temper was dangerously unstable. And although I hadn't been the object of his fury, I didn't know what he would say. On the other hand, this was my show. He was the one catching a ride. What he thought really didn't concern me as much as my absentminded slip-up did. The threat of a baby interfering with my ability to make the money I needed to bankroll my future scared the hell out of me.

I nervously finger-combed my hair. "I don't know. He's been so wrapped up in this book he's writing. I don't think he would notice."

Sensation took a bite of her cheeseburger. "Oh, when that money stops, boyfriend'll know something's wrong. He's gonna go berserk. All pimps do—"

"Let me stop you right there, boo-boo. Brody ain't no pimp," I said, almost yelling.

"Listen here, Miss Thang, you might want to believe that Brody is your man. But any man that will collect money from you at the end of the day sure isn't an altar boy. I mean, after spreading your ass over the street all night, at the end of the day all you get is a pat on the head and a kiss on the cheek. Baby girl, that's a pimp." She waved her plastic spoon around. "If it ain't, my name ain't Sensation. Please believe me."

"Like I said, nobody controls me," I told her firmly. Even though my sistah had absolutely no idea about my deal with Brody, I knew what role he was playing in this relationship. The deal was that I would bankroll the dough, and he would make me coauthor to the project. I loved Brody and all that, but our agreement wasn't much more than a business deal—for me, anyway. I wasn't gonna let Sensation talk me into believing that Brody was a pimp. I controlled everything.

"Is your man gonna give you the money to get an abortion or is he gonna take care of it the old-fashioned way?"

"What's that?"

"Beat it out of you."

I looked at Sensation like she had no sense at all. *Brody, hit me?*

"Big Sis—"

"Oh, it's Big Sis now? How much you wanna borrow?"

I couldn't touch the money I had in CDs because I didn't want to be stuck with a penalty fee. Plus, the little cash I had was strictly for situations. Granted, this was a personal emergency but why spend your own when you could borrow and pay back leisurely?

"It's just 'til Brody okays his second printing."

"Do you really think Brody has the talent to make it?"

"Do you really think I'd be on the streets if I didn't believe in him?"

Sensation was going to loan me the money. She'd come to my aid many times in the past. She glanced out the window and lit up another cigarette. Something was on her mind. I could tell. I followed her movements.

"Delicious, why doesn't Brody ever give you play money? It ain't like yo' hot little ass ain't popular on the track. You make tons of money, but you look like you still homeless."

"It ain't up to Brody to give me anything. I—" I put the brakes on the rest of my statement is what I did. I was here trying to borrow loot from her so that I didn't have to touch mine. The jig would be up if I let her know the real. So I played along. She didn't realize this was my show. I liked new clothes as much as the next woman, but nothing forces you to prioritize like having to spend a cold night sleeping under a freeway overpass. Clothes didn't mean that much to me. I was after big game, the elusive white rhino of security that could only be obtained with the almighty dollar.

"Denial is ugly. Delicious, you need to stop playing with yo' own mind, heifer, and wise up." Sensation was getting a little loud, so she calmed down and lowered her voice. "I'm gonna be blunt. Delicious, you look like shit. You probably could be doing thousands a week if you dressed yourself. But you can't 'cause Brody is pocketing all the money."

I was listening to what she was saying, but girlfriend didn't know the real deal. And I wasn't gonna highlight my plan. Women could be some of the biggest haters. I did believe in Brody's talent, however, I was seriously beginning to question his money management. He'd recently hooked up with a guy who was passing himself off as a publishing guru. My instincts told me that the short, fast-talking Jamaican man was a swindler. He was a low-class guy with a gift for selling high-class dreams. His attire, from the fancy suit that the older man wore down to the expensive shoes on his feet, reinforced his reptilian image. Brody was scheduled to pay him a ton of cash to start the publishing process. I tried to talk him out of it but Brody was so blinded by the con artist that he couldn't see the scam. We'd had a huge argument about the move and he'd promised he would go with somebody else. I was worried that Brody would do something stupid like break his promise and go swimming with that Jamaican shark.

"Delicious." Sensation gently rapped on my forehead. "Are you in there?"

"Stop, girl."

"Are you listening to me?"

"Your voice is carrying. How could I not be?"

Sensation looked away, and I saw her eyes widen, then narrow into slits. I had my back to the door, but I could tell that Big Sis seriously disliked whomever she was staring at. I slowly turned and saw Trixy enter. Lately, Trixy had been seriously craving our attention. We were two of the hottest girls on the track, which left Trixy's old ass bitter and very jealous. Last week, Trixy's pimp had gone upside her head because she wasn't bringing in much trap money. The word out on the track was that Trixy had had it with us and she was going to do something to one of us. She'd been seen brandishing a straight razor, bragging about slicing chunks of our faces off. Sensation had laughed it off. I, on the other hand, took any threat seriously. I had plans for my face when I was done with whoring.

"That bitch know she don't come in here to eat," Sensation said, puffing on her third cigarette.

Trixy ordered food and took a seat three booths away from us. She noticed us looking and gave us a sinister grin. But before I could say anything my attention was stolen by three figures who rushed in wearing ski masks, strapped with weapons.

"Everybody get the fuck on the floor!" the taller, huskier one ordered. "Nobody moves and nobody gets his wig shot off!" He moved to the cash register with the grace of a ballerina. One figure policed the dining area while another kept careful watch over the employees.

"That's them niggas I was telling you about," Sensation whispered.

"Shut the fuck up, bitch!" one of them yelled.

I hugged the floor like it was a john about to pay me double for doing such a wonderful job. I looked at Sensation. Her eyes were bugging out and her heavy breathing betrayed her terror. But what really bothered me, even worse than the lunatics waving guns around, was Trixy lying on the dirty floor smiling like she had come upon a lucky lottery ticket. I let it play out in my mind for a few ticks of the clock. It didn't take much detective work to figure out that her old stank ass was in on the robbery. She noticed me looking at her. Her old ass smiled wider.

My heart was pounding away. It seemed as if time had stood still, allowing these punks to do Satan's bidding. I'd seen scenes like this in movies and on news programs, situations where the gunman violently killed everyone after receiving the cash and goods.

I swallowed hard. I thought about Brody and the life that we could make together once he hit it big. Was this my last day on earth?

Just then the shorter one of the crew snatched Sensation off the floor by her ponytail.

"Look at this pretty bitch here." I could see his tongue wagging through the mouth slot of the mask. Gun in one hand, a fist full of hair in the other, the jerk perversely licked Sensation's trembling cheek. "You niggas gonna have to let a nigga get his freak on with this one."

He showed Sensation to his buddies. She shrieked with horror.

"We ain't got time for that shit," the figure at the cash register yelled. I assumed he was the boss.

"Leave that bitch alone," the third figure weighed in. This one was pretty chunky. "We after cash, not ass."

After the boss figure cleaned out the safe, he smacked the manager to his knees and promised that if anyone went toward a phone or stuck his or her head out of the door, he would blow it off. The thug who had Sensation by the hair looked at her and smiled.

"You better be lucky this is bidness." He licked her cheek again as though she was a chocolate sundae and flung her to the floor. Instinct made me look in Trixy's direction. I wasn't sure, but it looked like she was making head gestures toward me. The last thing I remembered was a high-pitched shriek, a sharp pain, then everything went black.

"Listen, Brody," I said into the phone. The three thugs who'd robbed the Coney Island restaurant had kidnapped me and were holding me in some sleazy motel. I had no idea where. I'd been instructed what to say and what not to say. I sat shivering, with a huge gun pointed at my temple, as I explained the situation to Brody. "Brody, I've…been…kidnapped…and the ransom is ten… ten grand." Brody started to speak, but the phone was suddenly snatched away from my ear.

"Listen, you little stank-ass pimp. I got this ho of yours and if you wanna see this bitch breathing again, I suggest you get me the money. Get cute, or call the police, and I'll cut this bitch up and mail you pieces of her for a month. Listen, nigga, you got one day, then I start mailing," the boss said in a harsh voice, slamming the phone down on the cradle.

A gag was placed over my mouth and my hands were tied with phone cord. Terrified, I looked around. Judging from the filthiness of the room, the thugs had been camped out for a while. Empty pizza boxes, wine bottles, and White Castle hamburger boxes were scattered everywhere.

As I watched my captors, I realized that I was a goner. The one that had snatched Sensation from the floor was looking at me like I would be fucked every which-a-way while they were killing me. He gave me the creeps most of all.

The shorter thug complained, "Man, how much fuckin' longer we gonna have to keep these mothafuckin' masks on? It's hot as a mothafucka in these bitches."

"Sit your stupid ass down and help me count this loot," the leader said. He was the tallest of the three. The black sweater he wore hugged his athletic physique as if he were born in the thing. "We got a few hours. I told ya'll niggas kidnapping these bitches was a moneymaker. These hoes make plenty of bread out on the track and those sucka-ass pimps will pay a pretty penny to get they merchandise back."

"How do you know her pimp is gonna pay for her?" the chunky one asked. This one was quiet, passive, like robbery and kidnapping were second nature to him. The third guy, the shorter one, seemed to be the baby of the group. He was whiny, impulsive, and unpredictable.

He pointed at me. "Have you seen this bitch on the track? She brings in that much in a week."

"You kiddin'?" the shorter one chimed in.

The leader tsked and poked a cigarette through the mouth of his mask. He lit it and through the smoke he said, "If the nigga know what's good for his bitch, he'll play ball. I promise you."

I should've been terrified and I was for the most part, but something about the leading man's demeanor put me at ease. It was the whiner I was worried about. The jerk had been freaky-breathing down my neck since the moment I'd woken up, looking at me like I was the last piece of steak on earth. I was seriously uncomfortable, and the baseball-sized knot on the back of my head throbbed and pulsated with every fearful beat of my heart.

"Why don't you lemme fuck this bitch while we waitin'?" Short and whiney asked like a petulant child.

"I told you to sit yo' stupid ass down and help me count this money!" the leader yelled.

Whiney dropped onto the bed I was sitting on and began fondling me, touching my pussy and roughly grabbing my breasts.

"Man, we might as well have some fun while we waitin' for this nigga to get dis money up. What ya say?"

The leader's moves were swift and smooth, almost blinding. Before I could blink, he'd backhanded the hell out of the shorter man. Whiny flipped off the bed and hit the dirty floor with a sickening *thud*.

"Fuck!" he hollered, jumping up off the floor. He charged at the leader like an angry bull. In a Steven Seagal kinda way, the bigger man sidestepped, catching the shorter one behind the head. Using his own body weight, he slung the little man hard against a wall. The shorter man crumbled in a heap on the floor. He gasped for air, then tried to get to his feet but helplessly slipped back to the floor. Blood flowed from his mouth.

The leader took a little time to catch his breath. "If you get back up, I'ma put it on your stupid ass some mo'."

The chunky one never stopped watching the baseball game. He showed absolutely no interest in the fight at all. The short thug had probably tested the bigger man many times before. In a way, they were kinda comical. But I made no mistake in believing that the leader wouldn't follow through with his threat if Brody didn't come up with the money.

As the hours ticked by, rolling swiftly toward the deadline, I made my peace with the Lord. I had no business doubting whether Brody would come through. After all, over the recent months, I'd earned the ransom money and more. Momma had also once told me that money had the power to turn the most righteous into fiendish, selfish slobs without a God-fearing conscience. I closed my eyes, trying to make sense of it all. But all I could think of was how badly my life was turning out.

I thought about praying but I wondered whether God would hear me. With all the dirt that I'd done and was still doing, I wondered whether God would care. I started to shiver. These goons had to have been watching me and following my every move. Something smelled fishy. And at the thought of fish, my stomach bubbled and my chest heaved uncontrollably. I threw up all over my gag, and the cheap comforter on the bed.

"Damn, that bitch blew chow." Whiney was quick with the play-by-play, still sitting on the floor, slowly rubbing the back of his head. "What the fuck's wrong with her?"

I heaved again. Nasty water spewed between the threads of the gag.

"Take that gag off her mouth," the leader ordered.

"Fuck dat," the shorter one retorted. "You take dat shit off her yo'self."

"You need some medicine?" the leader asked.

"Dat bitch need an exorcism. Fuckin' Linda Blair devil bitch," Whiney said, finally getting to his feet.

Boss Thug quickly cut my wrist restraints. I ran to the toilet, yakking along the way. I dropped to my knees, careful not to get too close to the filthy toilet bowl. It seemed as if my unborn knew that I was plotting its termination and was trying to escape before I had a chance to force it out. Then as quickly as the sickness came, it passed.

"You alright?" the leader's voice came from behind me.

Gasping, I said, "Just a little pregnant, that's all."

"Pregnant, hell," came Whiney's irritating voice. "Get yo' pregnant ass out here and clean this shit up."

"If I have to say something to you one more time," the taller one snarled in the short man's direction, "I'ma make sho' you'll be pickin' my shoe leather outta yo' ass for months."

"Whatever," Whiney said, throwing up his hands and taking a seat.

On the second day, the leader called Brody and instructed him on where to make the drop. Before he hung up, he once again warned Brody not to try anything shady or he would find my liver in our mailbox.

"Once we get the money we'll phone you and tell you where to pick up your bitch," Boss Thug informed Brody.

I was hogtied, gagged, and stuffed in a closet. All I could think about was Momma. What would she think if she could see her little girl? Kidnapped, tied up, and knocked up. The worst was yet to come. When I thought about how much of a whore I was becoming, more tears flowed. I had tried to pretend that the life I was leading was all one big television drama series and I was the lead actress. But no matter how many times I tried to lie to myself, I couldn't. The ten grand was sure to put us in the hole. I'd have to work the track beyond my projection for retirement. But I didn't care; I wasn't sure that I was going to work again. I wanted out of this fucking closet.

I could hear the television but there was no movement on the other side of the door. Some time had elapsed. I was zoning in and out when the door to the room slammed open. I almost jumped out of my skin. Had Brody come through? Were the thugs coming to get me and trade me for money? Had Brody reneged? Were they coming to kill me? My mind was buzzing. If they were coming to kill me, there was nothing I could do. I was ready to accept my fate and join my mother and father.

The closet doorknob rotated once to the right and twice to the left. Then the door was snatched open.

"Pumpkin, you all right?" Brody asked, leaning in to help me out. He quickly untied me and pulled the gag off. I could tell that he was pissed and relieved at the same time.

"Yeah, I think I'll make it." Without speaking, Brody led me out of the room and to the car, a hooptie we'd bought from a white man in Livonia two days before. Brody peeled out of the parking lot like a madman.

"Pumpkin, I'm sorry. I was supposed to be there, watching your back. You forgive me?"

I started to cry. "Yes. Brody, I was so scared."

"Nothing like that's gonna happen again. I promise."

I cried all the way home.


The middle of November was freezing cold. It'd been three weeks since the abduction and the tension in our home was palpable. Brody blamed me for delaying his project.

"Ten grand, Kimpa, ten-muthafuckin'-grand!" Brody screamed. "Do you know what that does to my project? It pushes the muthafucka back, that's what it does. Delays shit."

"What the hell you mean, *your* project? Brody, please. Have you ever stopped to think what I had to go through in that fucking closet? Not knowing if I would ever see the daylight again.

And since you so quick to blame me for shit, where were you when I was being kidnapped? Hunh?" My voice was on blast and I didn't care if the neighbors in the downstairs flat could hear me. I hadn't worked since the abduction and it was looking as though I wasn't going back. I kept having nightmares of waking up to masked men standing around the bed.

"You right." Brody calmed his voice. "I was supposed to be there. I got all this pressure on me to produce and I straight lost it. So, when do you think you going back to work?"

*The nuts on this nigga*, I thought.

"Brody, you didn't hear nothing I said. I'm scared. Every time I step outside this house I think somebody's waiting on me in the bushes, or at the corner, or at the market standing in the next aisle."

"Well, how the hell do you expect me to replace the ten grand? Pull it out my ass?"

I stood up from the couch and looked him straight in the eyes.

"Why not…I've been doing it," I said. He could hear the pain in my voice and see it in my eyes.

"Fucking hormones," he said, snatching his jacket off the couch, marching out the door, and slamming it so hard the front windows rattled.

I wanted to believe that I was experiencing a sudden overdose of paranoia, tried to tell myself that he was stressed because of the setback, but I could see the change in Brody's attitude as of late. The only time I would have any communication with him was when he came out of his study to eat my food. Afterward, he would give me a nasty stare and retreat to his study, slamming the door. He even had the nerve to tell me that I was holding him back; that if it weren't for me, he'd already be on a book tour. His ass was delusional. I don't mean to sound gross, but we were eating because of my pussy and if it weren't for me, the jackass would've still been crawling around through the garbage, looking for crumbs.

I still hadn't told Brody about my pregnancy. I had somewhat of a baby-bump and had to do something quickly. It was only a matter of time until my body completely gave up my secret. I couldn't keep hiding under oversized clothes or blame it on weight gain when he'd make inquiries in the shower. Given his present mood, I wasn't sure if I could bring it up. Sensation had promised me the money but her pimp had gotten locked up and she needed every dime to bail him out.

My eighteenth birthday was around the corner. Although I was young in age my body felt very old. I was paying a heavy price for our plans. I would give Brody another year. If he didn't produce by then, his ass was out of there. I was getting tired of the life. To make ends meet, I learned how to boost clothes from shopping stores during the day and finally, conquering my fears, I went back to the track.

I hadn't noticed it before but Brody was turning into a pretty snazzy dresser. He'd started improving on his usually sloppy appearance—keeping his Afro nice and neat, wearing an immaculate manicure and thick gold chain. My mind immediately rolled back to the comment Sensation had made about Brody's misappropriation of the money. She was right. I sucked and fucked, bearing all the shame, while he enjoyed the fruits. I really believed that the nigga was starting to buy into the whole pimp thing. He and I were going to have a little talk. I was going to have to bring his big helium head out of the sky by reminding him about our arrangement. I'd ingeniously crafted a way to lie on my back, entertaining my johns while dreaming of a fairytale land where life would be good for both of us, so blinded by fantasy that I didn't realize that Brody was focusing on the pimp role. Something was going to have to be done.

W e celebrated my eighteenth birthday at Red Lobster. On November 16th, eighteen years earlier, my mother had given birth to me. We ate dinner and wasted no time getting back home where I'd planned a quiet evening.

"What are you doing?" Brody scolded. He'd been drinking since the beginning of the day and now was stinking of cheap alcohol.

I was taking off my clothes and shoes, preparing to grab a shower. "What do you think?" This nigga and I were going to have a little talk about his attitude. He was twisted about his place on the food chain.

His lazy eye closed completely as he stomped toward me. "How many times have I told you not to answer my question with a question?"

"I thought we were going to chill and watch a movie." I went into my bag and grabbed the movie we'd rented at Blockbuster on the way home. "I thought we could cuddle up and watch *Boomerang.*"

To my horror, Brody smacked the movie out of my hand.

"Bitch, all that damn money I had to pay them sons of bitches. You better get yo' funky ass on the streets and make back what you lost. I'm twenty-five hundred away from the completion of my book." He smacked his left fist into his right palm. "Let me break it down to you—no twenty-five hundred, my book can't go to press. My book don't go to press, we can't get the big house with all the trimmings."

"Who the fuck are you—"

Brody bitch-smacked the hell out of me. His face turned into a mask of mean mad-dog wrinkles. I didn't even know him. The snarl on his lips warned me that if I didn't do what he said, I would be sorry for my disobedience.

My hand instantly searched my face. I could feel the spot marked by his paw print, pulsating and tingling. I went back at his ass, swinging wildly, but the nigga was too strong. A right hand sent me to the floor. The smack was so hard I couldn't produce tears. I was completely thrown off. My senses went haywire. He stood there staring down at me like he was getting off.

"Like I said, get out on that track or you gonna taste some real pain."

I couldn't believe it. I stood, defiant. Never before had he raised his hand to me. I figured if I wanted to establish some ground rules, I'd have to take a stand right here, right now. I was going to get my respect. This punk had it twisted. This was my show, I tried to convince myself, not allowing the tears to fall. I didn't see the closed fist that landed in my midsection. I folded like a cheap lawn chair. Brody kept up the assault. I was kneeling as though bowing at his feet. I saw the Northern Lights when the bastard kicked me in the head.

He huffed and puffed, trying to catch his breath.

"Got anything else you wanna say? Any mo' smart comments? It's time we get some shit established, Kimpa. I'm the brains and you're the booty. I said this before. If it wouldn't have been for you, I wouldn't be in the hole. So get up. Go wash yo'self up and get yo' ass out on the track."

I lay there, sniffling. My chest heaved in convulsions. Slowly I stood to my feet and stumbled to the bathroom. The door to Brody's study slammed.

My face was battered and covered with bruises that makeup couldn't begin to hide. I looked in the mirror; pain and grief stared back. I'd seen women who were misused by no-good-ass men. And I wasn't gonna be one of them. Yeah, Brody had gotten in a few cheap shots, but when things were all said and done, the muthafucka would owe me his manhood. I was hurt and there was no hiding it. I was confused and had no one to lean on. I didn't feel like listening to Sensation's I-told-you-so speech.

How could I get myself together? I needed to be held and reminded that everything would be alright. I was lost and didn't know what to do.

I needed to be somewhere else, 'cause if I stayed here, God only knew which one of us would be dragged out in handcuffs while the other was carried out on a stretcher amid the flashing lights from EMT trucks and police cruisers in full view of the nosy neighbors enjoying the nighttime entertainment.

I bundled up and walked out into the first snowfall of the season. It was blistering cold out. As I walked through the darkness, my mind struggled to kick-start my self-esteem. Why had God taken Momma away from me, leaving a little girl alone with the daunting task of learning how to become a woman? I had no other upstanding women in my life I could model myself after. Was I doomed to a life of misery, having cheap sex in third-rate motels and cars?

I had to pull myself together. I was a businesswoman with a degree in hustling. Brody had given me an ass whuppin'. Big deal. Right now I had to use my head. I put my personal issues aside and focused on business. I'd touched my face up so much that my heavy makeup made me look like a corpse in the restroom mirror of the Coney Island restaurant.

I bit down hard on my pride and took my place on the corner. I had to get money. My mission was made. I had to secure my future, even if it meant being abducted again. I had to hustle. Brody was going to pay, but right now I had to get paid. I took in a deep breath, trying to suppress the horrific pains in my stomach. By hook or by crook, I was determined to make it off this corner.

"What the hell happened to you?" Stan asked as we slid in the backseat of his Caddy. "Did Brody do that?" he asked, pointing to my face.

"We had an argument. Stan, I'd rather not talk about it. My

stomach is feeling kinda foul, so let's just get this over with. All right, sweetie?"

"Penny, that was more than an argument. Looks like he did all the talking with his fists. Won't you think about my proposal?"

He took down his pants, and I pulled down my thong and pulled up my dress. I straddled him.

"I guess there's no better time to tell you that I'm pregnant and you're the only one I let inside without a condom."

Stan relaxed his grip on my ass, the silence overwhelming. I was expecting for him to pull up his pants, toss me out on my ass, and burn rubber back to the 'burbs.

The white man surprised the hell out of me when he said, "How do you know that it's not Brody's?"

"Brody hasn't touched me in almost three months. You do the math."

"Are you going to keep it?"

"No, Stan. I won't have the baby. You know my situation. How would that look? Me takin' a baby that may or may not be Brody's back home. Not to mention it might be a mixed baby."

Stan slipped into the moment, breathing heavy and groping my booty again. He was breathing so hard he was fogging the windows.

"B-B-But he can put you on the street, right?"

"Stan, don't go there. We have an arrangement."

"Wait a minute," Stan said, his eyes popping open. "What the fuck? Either you're coming and don't know it or" —he pushed me up and hit the dome light—"you're having a serious miscarriage." Dark blood was everywhere.

"Shit! Stan, take me to the hospital!"

We wasted no time. Stan rushed me to the emergency room. He couldn't risk being seen, so he dropped me off and reluctantly left me alone.

During treatment the doctor asked about the bruises on my face: the black eye. My bottom lip was split and another nasty bruise stained my left cheek. I'd had a miscarriage, all right, resulting from the powerful punch in the stomach that Brody had given me. But I didn't tell the doctor that. I told him that I'd been walking home from the store and was attacked. The attacker was trying to rape me, causing the trauma to my face, but I fought back. The pesky doctor finally went away. I couldn't see him, but I realized that he was somewhere calling the cops. I was right. They'd showed up at my room in record time.

My beating became a police matter real quickly. They asked me a bunch of questions, including whether I'd gotten a good look at the suspect. I told them that the creep was wearing a mask. They kept trying to press me for information, kept looking at me suspiciously, like they weren't buying my story. I stuck to it. Even though I was tempted I wasn't gonna rat Brody's ass out. Sure, he'd put his hands on me, but I didn't think it was bad enough to send his ass to jail. After they asked more than enough questions, they left.

I lay in the bed and thought about how my life could've turned out had God spared my Momma. God, I thought. I had every right to hate Him. But I'd decided long ago that He gives us the choices. It's up to us to follow them.

"Wait on the Lord," Momma used to say. I wasn't about to wait any longer. I had to make it happen. I figured God had His powerful hands filled with the world, and was too busy to worry about my problems. My time was coming. One day God would come to see about me. But I would surprise Him with how well I'd done for myself.

I called Brody but got no answer. I kinda felt relieved. He probably was in his study writing. I tried him a few hours later. Nothing. I was puzzled. Brody never was one for ignoring the phone. Fear gripped me. Had those masked creeps come back to try to extort more money? I must've tried Brody all night. No answer. My mind was troubled. Just when I had given up and called the police, he picked up at five in the morning.

"Dammit, why you messing with my flow? You know I'm writing."

"I'm in the hospital."

The phone line grew quiet. I couldn't tell if the bastard was breathing. He was scared and I knew it.

"You didn't tell the police, did you?" his dumb-ass asked in a childish voice.

"I had a miscarriage, Brody." At this point I no longer cared about how he would react to shit. The baby wasn't his, but he didn't have to know. I tried to throw as much guilt as humanly possible at him; tried to behead him with it.

"Pregnant?"

I said nothing.

"Why didn't you tell me?"

"Brody—"

"Don't *Brody* me. Answer the question, Kimpa."

"The way you've been acting, would it have mattered?"

"It's troubling enough to know you could keep secrets from me."

"It troubles me that you could beat babies out of folks."

"Pumpkin, I'm sorry for putting my hands on you. I don't know exactly what came over me. Guess I'm just stressed with the book. I never should've harmed you. Can you find it in your heart to forgive a creep like me?"

"Brody."

"Yes?"

"They're releasing me later on this morning."

"Pumpkin, I'm on my way now." He hung up.

The following day I found out why it had taken so damn long for Brody to answer the phone. Sensation called me to put me up on the game.

"Delicious, you know I don't holds 'em up when it comes time to speak my peace. I'm only stepping to you because you claim yo' boy, Brody, is all about yo' coochie. And you know I'm not one for spitting venom on niggas, but yo' boy is foul," she said.

"Explain," I demanded, my voice firm.

"While you were laid up in the hospital last night, I saw Brody in the car outside ya'll's crib, lockin' lips with some bitch. I was coming out of a john's crib two doors down from ya'll's pad when I caught his ass tryna swallow the ho's tonsils."

"You sure it was Brody?"

"Bitch, are you listening to me? I know what that Forest Whitaker–looking nigga looks like."

I couldn't say shit. I froze up. Why should I care about who he was fucking? After all, it was only a business arrangement, right? I didn't even know why hot tears filled my eyes. Sensation was telling the truth, but I didn't want to believe that the man that I thought loved me could beat on me and step out on me at the same time. I didn't believe it. I remember Momma telling me to believe half of what's said and all of what's seen.

"You alright, girl?"

"Yeah, I'm tight. Just tired."

"You know I got yo' back."

"I know. Thank you, Big Sis."

"Well, this won't come as no surprise. Word from the ho-vine is that Trixy had something to do with you gettin' kidnapped and shit. I heard her broke ass is flossin' on the strip real hard—jewels, a mink, the whole nine. You know ain't nobody buying her polluted pussy for her to be flossin' like that. The ho can't even spell 'mink coat.' I heard she on the stroll talkin' real saucy about you and me. Them niggas broke her off a percent of the ransom money. Get some rest, girl, 'cause we gonna pay that trick a visit she'll never forget."

The next month of my life was pure hell. My doctor had advised me not to use my coochie for the next four weeks. Brody was beside himself with anger. There was so much stress and tension hanging around inside our house that it was suffocating. I slept in the bedroom while Brody slept on the couch. I rarely saw him, but when I did, he was irritable and on edge. Since I wasn't working, we had to dip into Brody's book money to pay some bills. I still had my account, but I wasn't gonna touch a damn thing. I could remember being homeless and sick with the flu; he went out to collect scrap metal to trade it for cash. He had hustle skills. If the bills were going to get paid, it was going to be on his hustle.

But when the transmission went out in the car, Brody flipped his wig and took it all out on me. I was called every bad name one ghetto child could possibly imagine. Brody would leave the house and wouldn't come back for days. And since he claimed that we had no more savings, I had no money to go buy groceries for the house. I didn't even feel guilty when I enjoyed a meal at the Coney Island restaurant. I had a little loot, but his ass had to eat the best way he could.

I received word that Stan was looking for me. One day when Brody went on one of his trips, I met Stan at the restaurant and he gave me a few dollars. We sat and talked for a few minutes. I didn't feel like hearing him tell me that Brody was a pig and that I was a princess who deserved to be treated accordingly. I took the money Stan had given me and purchased a few things for dinner from the grocery store. I was feeling pretty positive about myself and had plans to surprise Brody with a nice dinner.

As I seasoned my chicken legs, I struggled to unravel the mystery of Brody's elusive sex life. Before my miscarriage, Brody and I had been going through a dry spell. His reason was that he didn't want to wear out our future. He wanted to keep it nice and tight so that our tricks would be more than satisfied. My "freshness" would keep them coming back. He often made fun of his inhuman-sized dick—said if he kept on banging me, he'd make my coochie too big for all the tricks with small dicks. Brody was packin' and there was no doubt about it, but I seriously wasn't buying that crap. There was something else going on. In the back of my mind I imagined seeing him tonguing the bitch that Sensation had told me about.

The sharp snap, crackle, and pop of the cooking grease pulled me from my thoughts. I safely slipped a few legs into the hot grease, watching the flour take on a brownish color. I'd come to the startling realization that Brody had been hiding something.

I flipped the chicken over, put a lid on the skillet, checked my mac and cheese in the stove, and then I went to Brody's study. I didn't know what the hell I was looking for, but I rifled through Brody's file cabinet and searched his desk drawers. I found a photograph of us that had been taken at Club Entertainment. I was sitting in a wicker chair while Brody sat on one of the arms with his right arm draped around my neck. He was wearing one helluva Courvoisier smile. His alcoholic grin only matched my intoxicated, horny eyes.

When I picked up the photo, a bottle of pills behind it captured my attention. The prescription was for Valtrex. Valtrex was a medication for herpes. I'd learned that much from all the folks smiling brightly on the television commercials, like having herpes was something to be cheesing about.

The horror that gripped me was suffocating. My mouth ran dry and my palms dripped with nervous perspiration. I continued to examine the bottle as if the name of the medicine would change. My heart pounded out a frightening beat. The medicine was used to treat—I swallowed hard—*genital herpes*. The word "herpes" ran through my mind faster than a cheetah on speed. I felt a shiver run through me. I almost blacked out. I grabbed a seat at his desk.

Brody had herpes? All I could think about was the nights when we'd had unprotected sex. Those nights when I'd trusted his black ass. All types of thoughts flooded my head. Did I have it? I had to calm myself. I clicked on the computer and surfed the Internet for answers. I found what I was looking for. I pulled my knees to my chest, reading the information. The symptoms included groups of blisters that became open sores of raw exposed skin, or ulcers, which were extremely painful. The ulcers lasted from one to three weeks.

I stopped my reading to think. Put two and two together. I came up with the reason for our sporadic sex life—Brody was trying to conceal his shit. Whenever he'd have an outbreak, he'd put off sex. Didn't he know that herpes could be spread between outbreaks? Hadn't he seen those same commercials? And where the fuck did he get herpes from in the first place? That bitch he was kissing outside the crib, perhaps.

Enraged, I turned off the computer without going through the regular shutdown routine. My fists were clenched so tightly that my knuckles turned white.

"That sonofabitch!" I yelled. "How dare he put my life at risk!" It wasn't enough that I was putting my own life at risk out on the track; this nigga was exposing me, and cheating. The raw nerve! The ungrateful sonofabitch! I tried to remind myself of the business deal, but this nigga had gone too far.

The stench of burning chicken brought me back down to earth. I rushed into the kitchen. There were minor burns on the bird but those dark spots weren't gonna be enough to warrant the trash. I wiped my brow, not seeing Brody standing in the doorway watching me. I was so overwhelmed with rage, I forgot that I was still holding Brody's pill bottle.

"You've been going through my things?" Brody asked, staring insanely at my hand.

I looked at the bottle. I couldn't say anything. I was flat busted. Fear replaced my anger. The look that Brody wore danced on the borderline of insanity. He had a wild look in his eyes and wore a foolish smirk, but I had my hand on the handle of the burning hot skillet so I tightened my grip. The only other time I'd seen him look that way was when he abused crack.

I knew what was coming. No guesswork was needed. I wasted no time with words. I looked for an escape. I couldn't possibly take another drug beating.

"Nosey bitch." He pulled on his nose. "If your ass would've been on the track instead of wasting time thinking in this house, you wouldn't have been snooping." He coughed to clear his throat, raising his hands. "So now you know. What you gonna do?"

"Why?" I asked in an emotional voice, waving the pill bottle around.

"My business. Not yours."

I lost it. Truly lost it! My top lip quivered and my chest started heaving rapidly. Hot tears rolled down my cheeks uncontrollably. Not caring about Brody being twice my size and without having to think about it, I uncovered the hot skillet and threw the bubbling, skin-melting grease. I watched as the smoking solution and half-done chicken sailed at his face. The nigga had the reflexes of a cat alright. I didn't realize that he could move that damn fast. If the bastard's reaction weren't so swift, I would've caught all of his face and not just his neck.

The joker yelped with inhuman cries, screaming and dancing in pain as he shuffled through the house looking like a cartoon character, trying to find relief. His ass was on fire—and I mean that literally. I watched in open amusement as the fool ran through the house, smoking from the neck of his clothes, and right to the bathroom.

That was my break but instead of running out the damn door, my dumb ass went to the bedroom to pack a bag. It took me all of five minutes to get my shit together and start walking back through the kitchen. Sad mistake! In a rush, I forgot the damn grease on the floor. Next thing I knew, my foot slipped from underneath me and I went one way while my bag went the other. I hit the floor hard and rolled around in the grease, trying to shake out the cobwebs.

Wobbly, I finally struggled to my feet. Brody came from out of nowhere.

"Bitch!" he yelled, slapping me to the floor. "You done lost your mind!"

I looked up from the floor. His eyes were slits, totally devoid of anything remotely close to rational thinking.

"Muthafucka, why you didn't tell me you had herpes?" I screamed, sliding around in the grease on all fours.

The grease didn't seem as hot as it was when Brody had gotten a taste of it. I was eighteen but already had the mileage on my body of someone in her fifties, and I was fed the hell up. This nigga thought he was gonna get away with putting his hands on me. I'd just stepped out the hospital a month ago for this same treatment. I had already thrown my self-worth underneath a bus, traded it for a long-shot, and this fool thought I was gonna take his shit, too.

"I'ma kill you, bitch," he snarled, staying away from his old friend, the grease. It blanketed the floor, covering me and surrounding my body in a circular pattern, acting as some kind of force field. Brody's eyes were crazed, but he wouldn't come anywhere near me; the grease was a repellent. I guess he was shellshocked. Whatever it was, the joker had gained a healthy respect.

"You dead, bitch," he threatened again, holding on to the towel with tears in his eyes.

"Hurting, huh? Now you see what it feels like to be abused," I said, smiling and looking up at him. It was the funniest thing to see: Mister-Big-and-Bad standing his ground with me within reach, but not wanting to fall victim to the grease again. "Now let that bitch you were kissing in front of the house the night I was laying my ass up in the hospital put some butter on that burned-up neck of yours, playa—exposing me to herpes you probably got from that ho."

He said nothing; he stood there like he was trying to figure out a way to lure me from the center of my grease sanctuary.

"How about this for the title of your next book: I'm Leaving Your Punk Ass. Brody, are you smoking crack again?"

He groaned in pain. "You real funny with this grease between us. Ho, you gonna wind up like yo' momma, if I get my hands on you."

What did he say that for? I came out of my corner swinging. I picked up a chicken wing from the greasy floor and flung it at his head. Then I stood quickly while he dodged the flying wing and I rushed him before he had time to regroup.

The grease took away both of our footing as we bowled over

the kitchen table, him with his hands around my throat and me with my claws dug deeply into the burned skin of his neck. I was stripping away the towel from his neck when we slammed to the floor with all his weight on top, knocking the breath from my lungs. It took the fight out of me, almost causing me to lose consciousness.

"Bitch, I'll kill you," he said, both hands around my neck, straining so bad that a vein popped from the side of his neck. I felt myself going to sleep, when suddenly the front door to our flat was kicked open, followed by voices yelling "Police!" The lady downstairs must've called them after hearing all of the commotion. They ran in and grabbed Brody off of me.

I'll be damned. It happened exactly like I'd predicted a month ago. Only I didn't know right away which one of us was going to jail and which one was going to the hospital. My question was answered when the cold bracelets were snapped around my wrists as the police led me out into the night air in front of a crowd of curious neighborhood folk and the flashing lights from police units and an ambulance. The EMTs brought Brody out afterward on a stretcher. He was cussing, still calling me a bitch and yelling about how much pain he was in.

I'd gone a round with Godzilla and my reward for surviving was a cruise downtown to the county jail. I was taken to lockup, fingerprinted, photographed, and charged with aggravated assault. It didn't matter to me, though. I was placed in a holding cell. I didn't know what was in store for me; I'd never run afoul of the law before. But I knew one thing: I'd stood up for myself and Brody was history. Tina had her Ike and I had Brody. I'd left my mark on that bastard in the form of second-degree burns, blisters, and melted flesh.

I was given one phone call. Stan came down in a jiffy. I couldn't believe that during all the conversations we'd had, he'd never told me that he was a personal defense attorney. I was arraigned the very next morning and released on a personal. I smelled sour and seriously not clean. My head was blazing with pain from trying to sleep on the slab of concrete that passed as a bed. And on top of it all, the Old Lady was threatening. I was cramping and in no mood for foolishness.

Stan had on a nice caramel-colored overcoat, same color hat, and galoshes. He explained my situation to me on the way back to the neighborhood.

"I know the prosecuting attorney handling this case, play golf with him, and he owes me a ton of favors. I can try to get this thing tossed as self-defense. You have no priors, so the worst you could get out of this is a slap on the wrist—probation and community service."

I don't know where it came from but a chuckle broke through my lips.

"What's so funny?" Stan wanted to know as we jumped on I-94.

"I already serve the community."

"I want to talk to you about that," he said, unfazed by my self-denigrating attempt at humor. "You have to stop. You assaulted a man with hot cooking grease. I'm sure that's entertaining for Tyler Perry movies but this isn't *Madea's Family Reunion*. You have to keep your nose clean. If you get busted for prostitution, the courts aren't going to be so forgiving the next time."

"Can you tell me what to do?" I said, the tears coming slowly, my hair standing up on my head. "'Cause I don't know anymore." I was tired of my life. Just felt like taking a handful of sleeping pills to cure my misery. I felt like borrowing from the movie *Misery* and going all Kathy Bates on Brody's ankles with a sledgehammer.

"Okay, Kimpa Peoples," Stan said with sarcasm.

"Stan, you have to understand that I couldn't give you my real name, right?"

He smiled, reminding me of a mid-forties' William Shatner. "Yes. I understand. By the way"—he extended his hand—"pleased to meet you, Kimpa Peoples."

"Alright, Stan Larkin, Jr.," I joked.

"You want to talk about a brother's last name. You got jokes?" He laughed it off.

"You may be somebody's brother, but you are not a *brotha*," I came back.

His warmth made me smile. But what I was thinking was seriously wrong. I wanted Brody dead and all I had to do was ask Stan for the loot. I could make it happen. Of course Stan wouldn't ask me any questions about why I needed it. And I wouldn't tell him either. This shit would be between Brody's punk ass and me; I could meet up with a hitman in some stinking alley to arrange the hit. That was one thing about the nature of my business: cold-blooded killers were a surplus in the 'hood. But this was all a fantasy. I needed Brody's dark-hearted ass.

"Okay, in all seriousness. Here's what we're going to do." Stan exited the freeway at Joy RD. "I'll put you up in a hotel until you can get yourself a job. All you have to promise me is that you don't go back to Brody. I'm afraid the next time you might not be so lucky."

"But what about going to get my stuff?"

"I'll get you set up and then I'll give you an allowance to replace the stuff you lost—deal?"

"Okay. But only until I get on my feet." Stan had officially become my Plan B. "Stan, can you get me some muscle relaxants, please?"

"Something wrong?"

"No. I'm fine."

"Okay. I'll see what I can do."

The next day I was back on the track. I'd promised Stan that I would stay away, but I had to holler at my girl, and put her up on what had gone down between me and wannabe pimp, King Tito. We were clowning. It wasn't really funny at the time, but my story of how I'd tried to melt that bastard's skin off his neck with the hot chicken grease drew side-splitting laughter from the both of us. And of course she almost died when I told her that Stan had bailed me out and given me a roll of cash to go shopping with.

Sensation and I were going to have a girls' day out—pampering, getting our hair and nails done, facials, massages, tearing up the malls for hot sales. I was cramping badly, but the Old Lady wouldn't get me down.

I had a new direction, money in CD accounts, and a fat wad of cash in my pockets. Plus, I had awakened that morning in the lap of luxury. Stan had put me up at the Ritz-Carlton in Dearborn. There was nothing more refreshing than a bubble bath with scented candles, sipping on crystal flutes of champagne, and eating lobster tails. I explained everything to Sensation as we walked, about to go get something to eat—my treat—from Coney Island when we saw the bitch Trixy walking with her posse.

A light snow was falling. Fortunately for us, none of the stuff was sticking to the ground. I needed all the traction I could get while flexin' on the old bag. True to the streets, the ho was rocking the mink jacket and some fly-ass jewels, but the ghetto tramp had the raggedy nerve to have on some of those Timberlands that came up to the knee. No class at all. Not even mink material. But it didn't matter; her ass was all mine.

My big sister and I glanced at each other. We'd been together for a while now and she was up on my thoughts. Trixy was so busy being adored by her girls, she didn't even see us sneaking up on them like five-o.

She rolled her neck, her nappy weave ponytail blowing in the breeze.

"Ya'll hoes got beef?" she asked with acid in her voice.

Her girls got the drift, turning to face us like we were supposed to fall back and run or something.

"Bitch!" I shouted. "When you rob a nigga, make sure you keep it off the ho grapevine!"

"Ho, you gots problems now," Sensation added. "So hand over the coat or we're gonna stomp yo' stretch-marked old ass into a coma."

"Oh no, she didn't, boo-boo," one of her posse said, but she shut all that hostile shit down when Sensation went into her Dooney, pulling her pistol.

"If you bitches want to keep on working the track, ya'll better get to steppin'," Sensation warned them, pointing the pistol.

Those skanks cut the corner real quick.

"Yeah, it was me, bitch. I set you up and now I wish Alonzo 'nem would've killed yo' ass," Trixy said. "Why don't you put the gun down and fight fair?"

"No problem," I said, taking my coat off, handing it to Sensation. I stood in front of Trixy, mean-muggin'. The tramp had cost me ten grand and an ass whuppin'. She was going down. Trixy didn't even see it coming. Quicker than the eye could see, I produced the surgical scalpel I'd bought earlier from a crackhead nurse to protect myself from Brody.

Trixy froze. Her eyes grew bigger than silver dollars. Before she could react I sliced her face; one long, thin, bloody red line that started from her right jaw and traveled clean across her nose to the left side of her face. The bitch yelped almost like a wounded dog and tried to make tracks, but Sensation wasn't buying it. She tripped up the bimbo, and Trixy fell hard to the cold street. After that, I dropped the scalpel and stomped the brakes off her monkey ass, stripping the mink off her back and throwing it right in the pathway of an approaching bus.

I spit on her.

"Bitch, remember this the next time you try to have somebody jacked." I picked up the scalpel and chucked it down the sewer.

"And next time you rob somebody, get ya damn nappy-ass weave done," Sensation said, laughing, dapping me, putting her pistol back in her purse.

Yeah, I was laughing now. But as my anger melted away I remembered Stan's warning about keeping my nose clean. I wasn't a whole day out of lockup and I'd already assaulted somebody with a lethal weapon. That's when I got scared. If Trixy went to the police and pressed charges, I'd be packed away, the property of a women's correctional facility. I was a criminal.

I hadn't seen Brody in a few weeks. I still kept my appointments with my regulars but I made them spring for hotel rooms. The conditions of my bond left no room for more run-ins with the law. I had a court date coming up in two weeks and I'd been warned to stay away from Brody. I was bored and lonely, tired to death of meaningless sex. I wanted to be held and caressed, told that everything would be alright, even if it was a lie. I needed to hear it; it was something that I couldn't get from a paying customer.

I hated to admit it but I was missing Brody. How could I miss somebody who only cared about himself? Regardless of his reputation, Brody had a sweet side. I missed his big, strong embrace.

Sensation called me the other day, letting me know that Brody had been on the track looking for me. She said boyfriend was looking real bad, too. She laughed, describing him as unshaven, with sad, drooping eyes, and said that he had apparently lost weight. She said he looked like he'd been back sleeping out on the streets. Sensation joked about his burned neck. She compared his gross skin to Freddy Krueger's. My heart went out to him. After all, the man had his good qualities, and we'd had some good times together.

I loved Brody dearly. And I'm sure he loved me, but I wasn't gonna let him use me as a punching bag, or batter my face while he worked through his stress or childhood issues. I was flattered that Stan had been paying my way and handling my case pro bono. But I needed something more stable. Nothing that wasn't your own lasted forever. I needed my own.

My intuition was telling me that Brody's project was going to blow, and I deserved to be compensated for all my hard work in helping him to succeed. He owed me big. One day I would give him a phone call, but not right now. Stan had me living like a queen. I was pampered and becoming a little spoiled with room service, shopping sprees, my nightly ritual of sitting in a tub of bubbles, aromatherapy, sipping champagne, and eating lobster. It was all about me right now. Brody needed to be punished and I didn't see no harm in letting that big water-head joker sweat for his crimes.

I almost jumped into Stan's arms and straddled him when the judge banged his gavel, clearing me of all charges. But the old, white, wrinkled, prune-faced, bifocal-wearing judge read me the riot act about the severity of throwing hot grease into somebody's face. He informed me that he'd just judged a case like mine where a woman had doused her husband in the face with acid. After the jury found her guilty, he didn't have any gripes about handing out a stiff fifteen-to-twenty-year sentence.

The celebration was short-lived when Stan dropped a bomb on me about how his wife had gotten a hold of one of his credit card statements and had jumped all over him about the hotel room. Somehow the broad had bribed one of the front desk clerks into telling her exactly who was staying in the room. The heifer had threatened to divorce Stan and take custody of the kids, and him to the cleaners, if he didn't put an end to his affair with "that nigger whore"—her exact words. Anyway, Stan broke the news to me that he couldn't continue to honor his part of the deal.

"You can stay at my house long as you need to," Sensation offered, driving all that I had accumulated over to her apartment not too far from the track.

"Thanks, Big Sis, but I think it's time for me to have that talk." Sensation's Honda Accord was pretty nice. It was secondhand but cute. "I might need to keep all my new stuff over your house. Don't need no more drama."

"I hear you. By the way, word on the track is that Trixy copped a bus ticket and bailed to Atlanta somewhere. You won't have no mo' trouble out of girlfriend."

I said nothing as I watched the snow fall off the windshield in huge, clumsy-looking flakes. I looked out on the ghetto. It was ugly. I was tired. The bags under my eyes told my tale.

"I don't know about this, Delicious. Do you think you can trust him? I mean, how do you know that he's not gonna nut up again?"

"Brody has learned his lesson. I'm just ready to move on."

"That's cool and everything, but them types you can't trust."

I turned to look at her.

"What yo' Rihanna-looking ass staring at?"

"You, heifer. I don't say shit when Boss be going upside yo' head."

"Ouch, you cow. Excuse me for being concerned."

"I didn't mean nothing by it. Just tired, that's all."

"So where does he wanna meet you to talk?"

"Dining Time restaurant."

"Damn, brotha-man trying to make an impression. That's the spot with the mile-long waiting list every time I go down there. It's expensive as hell, too. *You go, Brody.*"

"Listen at you. Can you drop me off down there?"

"On one condition."

"What do you want?"

"Let me wear those cute brown shoes you got from Macy's and you got a deal."

"Whatever. Don't stank up my shoes, have 'em smelling like funky corn chips."

We laughed all the way to her apartment and unloaded my junk. I got dressed and Sensation took me to the restaurant.


I made sure I was looking cute. I'd had my hair done a couple days ago, the curls surprising me by holding so long. They usually dropped by now. Cherry-red lipstick painted my thick lips. My DKNY pantsuit was showing off my curves and my succulent thighs. I didn't want to toot my own horn but baby girl was generously stacked in the back. A table filled with brothers stood in open admiration of what my momma gave me as I scooted through the crowd eating up the attention.

The dining room was crowded; there was not one empty table. The room was vibrant with elaborate color schemes, crispy white table linen, globe-shaped candleholders, and low lighting. A small bandstand featured a live band playing smooth jazz music, giving the spot a touch of elegance. I melted, loving this kind of treatment. Being catered to is every woman's desire.

I was grooving to the band when I heard a voice from behind me. "You look beautiful, Pumpkin."

I went to return the compliment until I looked around and almost screamed.

Brody saw the horror in my eyes.

"I know"—he bent, kissing me on the forehead—"yeah, I know. Looks pretty bad, but the doctor assured me that I have a chance at a full recovery." From behind his back he pulled a dozen long-stem roses. "These are for you, Pumpkin." Despite his neck, Brody was handsomely dressed in a royal blue blazer, black slacks, and loafers, smelling of Cartier cologne.

He took a seat across from me. I still couldn't believe the destruction that I'd caused this man. Tears instantly welled in my eyes at the sight of his neck. I hated to say it but Sensation's Freddy Krueger comparison wasn't even in the ballpark. The last time I'd seen something burned so badly, it was a hotdog I'd let the fire get to on the grill.

I tried to say something but my words stuck in my throat. I tried to offer him an apology but all I could do was stare through tear-blurred eyes.

Brody came to my rescue.

"Pumpkin, it's alright. I mean, I was acting like an ass and deserved what I got. There was a lady on the news who'd thrown acid in her husband's face, and I came out better than he did."

"Does it hurt?"

Brody cracked a grin. I tried not to glare.

"Yeah, it hurt like a mickey-flickey. But I'm tough." He examined me, his eyes roaming, devouring me, and asking forgiveness. "Baby, what happened? How did we get to this point? I want you to be candid as possible."

I waited for the waiter to take our drink orders before answering. The waiter did something that I thought was awesome. He took my roses and brought them back in a pretty glass vase, sitting it in the middle of the table.

"Thank you," I said, smiling and feeling like a princess. The waiter left. "You turned into the mack, Brody. The business arrangement was that you'd watch over me while I made the money. But you totally flipped the script." The waiter returned and I waited for him to place our drinks. He took our dinner orders and bounced. "Brody, I'm sorry for your neck, but when you put your hands on me, I lost it."

Brody let his gaze drift to a couple being seated. The band had stopped playing, taking a short break.

"Some doctor has the idea that I'm bipolar. He has me on Zoloft. It's a...um...anti-anxiety medication. Baby, I let the stress get to me. I'm sorry. Please forgive me."

Bipolar. It explained why this joker was mentally switching gears every other day. I didn't know if I should buy into his craziness. If he was nuts, the medication would help. But right now he did look kind of bananas asking for my forgiveness after I'd microwaved his neck.

"Can you promise me no more fighting? I can't take it, Brody. We supposed to be working together, not trying to kill each other." I took a sip of my lemonade. I wasn't quite legal so lemonade was the strongest drink on the menu for me.

Brody smiled as a few people stared rudely. His wounds were gaining a few spectators.

"Yes, Pumpkin, I promise. And I have a surprise for you." He went inside his jacket and removed a book. I almost jumped to the ceiling when I saw his handsome face gracing the back of the jacket cover. He had a turtleneck on to hide the burns.

"Your book. God, Brody, this is wonderful! When did it print?"

"This is a promotional copy. We get the rest in a few weeks. I already got a distributor and local stores are lining up for a piece."

"I'm so proud of you. I knew you could do it. The cover is beautiful—and look, there's your name. I'm so happy for you—"

"No. Look carefully at the book."

I almost jumped from my chair. My name was right next to his.

"You kept your promise." I smiled hard enough to crack the skin on my forehead.

"You're happy for *us*. *We're* on our way."

"Brody, how long have you had herpes?" I took the wind right out of his sails with that one.

Brody took a moment to answer. He simply gave me that "You sure know your way around taking the excitement out of good news" look.

"Pumpkin, I screwed up. But please don't leave me. Our dreams are about to happen. Please don't leave me. I'll do anything. There are plenty of ways to keep you from contracting it. Please—"

I rushed from my chair and kissed him on the lips. He had me at Pumpkin.

Brody believed that a good marketing plan would push his book right to the top. The book was titled *The Truth Before Death*. And when the finished copies finally came, I was in awe. Brody didn't go with the original cover he'd shown me at the restaurant that night but the new cover was slamming. It wasn't until then that I had a chance to skim through the book. Brody was very superstitious and didn't believe in telling anybody about his story before it was published. When I really sat down to read it, I was blown away. Boyfriend had some serious skills. The story was about four young men who had witnessed a brutal murder perpetrated by a black mafia family. The shooter recognized the four young boys, and instead of killing them, he made them promise to never talk about what they'd seen. Years later, one of the three boys decided to become a writer and brought the secret to life in the pages of his novel. The young boy might've forgotten about the past, but the killer never forgot about the promise of killing the four boys if they told. Even though life had taken them to different parts of the country, the past would hunt them down. One by one, the killer bumped them off, saving the big-time author for last. What follows was a chase across the country with the author moving from one state to another trying to stay alive.

The writing was a revelation. It was as close to real as real could get. Reading the story made me feel that Brody was the writer who'd opened Pandora's Box. At that moment, a cold chill touched me.

"Oh my God," I said to myself, staring at the cover of the book. "I can't believe how silly I'm acting. This is just a work of fiction."

The book blew up. It was a smash. Folks in Detroit couldn't get enough. Brody was a featured guest on radio programs around the city. We peddled books from the trunk of the car. He targeted all the major hair salons around town and sold books at festivals. The car had become our office.

I didn't know if I was falling deeper for Brody or the idea of being rich beyond my wildest imagination. We were a team, working as one. The ride to this point had been rough and filled with much skepticism. And even though I hadn't written down one single word, I felt entitled to my name being alongside his. I wasn't the author, but I damn sure had lain between the covers so he could afford to write the pages. From a morality stand-point, the price was incomparable. It could probably end up costing me my eternal soul. So, damn right I should've been broke off a little sumptin'-sumptin'.

The promotional strategy he'd sent to a few of the main book distributors in the state worked like a charm. Our book was picked up and distributed throughout the country. I didn't want to come off like a fraud in the interviews so Brody coached me on his most intimate thoughts while he was penning this jewel. We received requests for appearances in every major city. We were red hot. We started doing book signings everywhere. And as the money started slowly coming in, our lifestyle took us from a two-bedroom flat to a ranch home in West Bloomfield. I'd asked Brody about Southfield but he told me that the city was going to be the next Detroit soon.

Our sudden wealth made the people in our small circle green with envy. It hurt me to my heart knowing that Sensation was one of them. Girlfriend started acting funny and stopped return-ing my phone calls. The word on the track was that she'd been spittin' venom on my name, calling me dumb and stupid. She was spreading my dirty laundry on the track to make me look bad, using information that I'd told her in confidence. Even though some of the stuff was true, she didn't have to tell the other girls.

But I wasn't going back—an option she didn't have—so I didn't care. Like I said before: women could be some of the biggest haters when it came to one of us getting ahead.

By mid-May, we'd sold over forty thousand copies. Not bad for self-published authors. The book debuted at number three on the *Essence* Bestsellers List for paperbacks. *The Truth Before Death* was the hottest gossip in every city. We'd even gotten a few offers from the motion picture industry.

Brody had kept his promise for the most part. He didn't hit me or otherwise abuse me. But I could tell that, with our demanding schedule, it was only a matter of time before he would start using. Brody wasn't an abuser, but he'd use the stuff to take the edge off when he was stressed.

For the most part, I liked being on the road, bouncing from city to city, people clamoring over us for a picture at book signings. Our dreams were finally coming true. We had the house that we'd dreamed about, two brand-new cars to drive around town in, and lots of jewelry. The house was huge: six bedrooms and four bathrooms, a spacious kitchen, stainless steel appliances, a gorgeous spiral staircase, a huge family room, and a foyer with marble tile. The thing sat on two acres of land, with a nice in-ground swimming pool that I would have to take lessons for since I wasn't a very good swimmer. In addition to playing interior decorator, I now pampered myself crazy with my daily ritual of aromatherapy, having stepped up my game from a regular bathtub to Jacuzzi bubble baths, lobster, and champagne. I flossed around town in my black BMW 745, mostly running errands for Brody.

One year later we had done the unthinkable: two homeless people had stepped from the stinking alleys of downtown Detroit to capture wealth, fame, and dignity. Our stories had been told in most of the urban magazines and scores of inner-city newspaper columnists couldn't get enough of our rags-to-riches story. I was nineteen and loving our affluent lifestyle. And I was three months' pregnant. Any other time this would've been a joyous occasion, time to break out the bubbly and toast to all the hard work that had gone into our climb from the gutter. I still didn't trust him. I hadn't gotten over the trauma from losing my last baby to a miscarriage. Brody might've had money, but he was still an unpredictable, mean and hateful bastard. I was determined not to lose this baby. I had to protect my unborn and if hiding it from Brody until I was ready to disclose those facts was the way to go, then so be it. But Brody made it easy to hide my baby in plain sight. He was far too busy to even notice me lately. He'd seen me naked in the shower a couple times and called me a fat-ass cow, pointing to my pooch, scolding me for not keeping my body tight. He told me just because I wasn't on the track anymore wasn't a sound reason for letting myself go. Brody was even cold enough to warn that I'd be out on my ass if I didn't do something about my weight gain.

Brody had undergone plastic surgery to improve the appearance of the skin on his neck and was putting together plans for another potential chart-topper. I wanted to give him his fame so I stayed off the project. Surprisingly, I'd recently found that I had some serious skills of my own. I'd started keeping a journal of my life, trying to date it back to when we'd first made the arrangement. All the time I'd spent on the road pretending had really given me the bug.

The attention I received was always welcome until someone

would raise the question of my next project. Those questions would have me feeling like a fraud at first, until running into some of my old tricks would remind me that I furnished this lifestyle entirely with my hustle. If you wanna be technical, Brody was the hitchhiker.

I was thinking about taking classes at Oakland Community College, possibly some creative writing courses. Brody was going to have something to say, but it would be of little importance to me. I was investing in myself. He would argue that one writer in the family was enough, but it was all a smokescreen. My take on it was that he didn't want the competition.

I couldn't believe my spiritual transformation. Indeed God had blessed us, so I decided to give Him some of my time. I'd been picking up my Bible, and had even attended a few services at the Baptist church around the corner. I had never belonged, or even been to a predominantly white church before. When I first walked into the church, I felt a bit uneasy. Church was supposed to be a place where fellowship transcended race. Every culture was bound together under one Supreme Being. One God. But I didn't feel that way. When I went to sit down, I felt the eyes searching me, probing me for some insecurity they could exploit. But I would hold my head high and enjoy the service.

I tried to keep busy while Brody was in L.A. I stepped out of the car and walked into the house. It was a scorcher of a day and my outfit revealed more skin than material. I'd just come from my manicure and pedicure appointment when the phone rang. I was expecting to hear Brody's voice. He'd been in L.A. for the past two weeks, negotiating with an independent production company for the movie rights. He was due back later.

The phone rang again.

"Hi, baby. I'm glad to hear…"

"Where the fuck is that fat nigga of yours?" a deep, eerie voice asked.

I looked at the phone like it had turned into a snake in my hand. "Who is—"

"Shut up and listen, bitch. Tell that nigga that he broke a promise. Now he has to pay the price." The caller hung up.

I swallowed hard as the dial tone buzzed in my ear. A yellow strip of fear crawled up my back. My jaw hung loose as if it had been torn from my face but was left dangling by paper-thin tendons. Usually prank calls didn't get to me. But this hair-raising voice held conviction. A promise of destruction. I rushed around checking all the doors and windows, making sure they were locked and bolted. I wanted to call Brody, but didn't want to worry him. Besides he would've just boarded his flight.

Something creaked behind me. I almost jumped out of my skin, turning completely around to see if somebody was behind me. I felt butt-stupid when I remembered that whenever the central air came on, it always made the floor creak. The phone rang again. I jumped in that direction. My thoughts were focused on the ominous threat. Against my will, I pushed myself toward the phone, taking baby steps. It seemed to be the longest walk of my life.

"Hello," I timidly answered.

"Hey, baby, we did it!" Brody yelled in excitement.

"Did what?"

"I sold the movie rights of *The Truth Before Death* to Starline Pictures for half a million dollars, and I also negotiated for a percentage of box office sales."

"That's good," I said, looking around uneasily.

"That's good? That's great! I want you to put your best dress on because tonight we're going to celebrate."

"Brody, have you landed?"

"No. I'm calling from the plane. We're about to taxi away from the terminal in L.A. I should be landing in a few hours. We'll celebrate over dinner. Baby, we're going to be rich."

"Brody—"

"Well, I gotta go."

"Brody."

"See you when I touch down. Bye."

"Brody."

He hung up.

Okay, I had issues. During dinner, I tried to tell Brody about the phone call, but he kept on raving about the success that had been long in coming. I couldn't get a word in. He went on about the lifestyle that he was going to live when the movie deal went through. The Negro kept on, not bothering to listen to me.

Since the threatening phone call, I'd been on high alert. Everything that looked suspicious sent my stomach into knots. I must've jumped at every little thing, everything from doors slamming to silverware clanking too loudly against dinnerware. I hated sitting with my back to the door. The way Brody was swinging on his own vine made me feel that if some masked creeps did come through the door blasting, Brody would hit the floor without warning me. He would leave me to pay for his sins.

Being at the hottest restaurant in town didn't make me feel any safer. The Supper Club was trendy. It sat on Jefferson Avenue, in the middle of downtown Detroit. The place was always busy;

the hour-long waiting list was proof. Anybody could've walked out of the crowd shooting.

The intoxicatingly rich aroma of Brody's barbecue ribs met us long before the waiter set our entrées down. The ranch dressing topped my grilled chicken salad like a snow-capped mountain.

Brody finally got off his high horse and asked, "What's wrong with you?" I guess he'd observed the way my fork shook while I tried my best to pick up my food.

"Just a little tired," I lied. I don't know why I lied. I gave up my one chance to tell him about the threatening phone call. Brody was so busy with writing that I didn't want him to be worried, but I had to give him the heads-up.

I cleared my throat and was ready to tell him when his cell phone vibrated. He politely excused himself from the table. It wasn't that he had manners; my guess was that he didn't want me to hear his conversation. I was perfectly fine with that. His absence gave me enough time to reflect on my own personal dilemma: I was three months' pregnant. I didn't know how Brody would react and except for the threatening phone call, everything was going wonderfully. But I would be lying if I said that I wasn't afraid. The asshole had already been responsible for my miscarriage. He'd killed one baby. I didn't know what I would do if he tried again. No matter what he said, I was gonna have my baby. And if he thought that that hot grease bath was painful, it would pale in comparison to what he'd get for messing around with the cub of a mother grizzly. We were sitting on big bucks now, not married, and Brody knew that a baby would give me power. So I had to be careful. The nigga could be more dangerous than before.

As the hostess walked an elderly couple to the back of the restaurant, my eyes followed them. When they turned a corner, my gaze shifted to a man sitting a few tables away. Normally I'm not one to stare, but his dark sunglasses left me curious as to whether he was blind or bad-mannered. He met my stare over the top of his shades; I felt a chill pass over me. Only one eyebrow arched over the glasses—the other was noticeably missing. The look of recognition this guy was giving me was pretty creepy.

I began to wonder what was taking Brody so long to return. I got up from the table, walked past a server's station and stumbled into a server, almost knocking his tray of salads and breadsticks from his hand.

"Oops," I said to the male server, trying to downplay the embarrassment. "I'm very sorry."

Brody's laughter, mixed with soft female giggles, came from the area of the restrooms.

When I made my way past the kitchen doors to the restroom area, I was literally sick to my stomach. Brody was holding hands with some white chick, laughing and giggling like a horny schoolboy. He didn't see me so I stood there, waiting to see how long he was going to hold her hand. I couldn't believe that he was openly flirting with this Angelina Jolie wannabe.

"I'm glad you enjoyed the book," Brody told her, smiling like he wanted to jump her bones.

"I can't wait until the next one comes out," she said in an irritating, high-pitched, Betty Boop voice.

Brody moved in a little closer. "If you like that, then you're going to love it when the movie comes out."

"A movie!" she exclaimed, dramatically snatching her hands away from Brody's and covering her mouth. "Can I be in it? I mean, can you talk to the director and get me a screen test?"

Brody smiled like he was Hugh Hefner. "Absolutely."

"I mean, I'm a natural actress. And as you can see" —she stepped back, shoving one hand in the air and whirling around on her stilettos like she was a supermodel— "it's not like I don't have the body." The fake broad was wearing a strapless designer dress. Granted, the dress was classy, but the white-trash bimbo was first-class junk mail.

"Lawd have mercy," Brody replied, taking her hand again.

Anger exploded inside me, but I tried to hold it together. I didn't want to jump the gun too fast. So far, all I had was a little harmless flirting going on between a wannabe superstar and a jock-riding hoochie.

My anger turned to venom when Brody ran his hand up the length of her arm and caressed her pasty cheek.

"The way you looking," Brody said, "you can get the leading role. Just give me your number and—"

I angrily cleared my throat so loud that a short man coming out of the bathroom turned his head in my direction, along with Brody and the bimbo.

"Hi, honey." Brody tried to play it off. His eyes were wide with surprise. "This is—uhh—what is your name again?" he nervously asked.

"Tiffany. Tiffany Zesty." Tiffany smirked, looking up at Brody, and then rolling her eyes in my direction. She knew the score. She looked at me, her blue eyes teasing, trying to make me jealous. She took a card from her purse. "Here, Brody, call me." She shook his hand one more time, cut her eyes at me, popped her lips, and strutted off, leaving Brody looking like a little boy caught with his hands in the cookie jar.

"She was just—"

"Save it!" I yelled.

"Like I said, she was just complimenting me on the book."

Now it was my turn to pop my lips. I folded my arms across my chest, shooting Brody a dirty look.

"Save that sorry shit for your mama," I said with tons of sauce.

"Pumpkin, that was nothing. I swear it. It wasn't what it looked like."

"Take me home right now!" I yelled, drawing attention. But I didn't give a damn. Brody had disrespected me and if I let this shit slide, he'd be physically punching on me in no time.

"But, baby..." he tried to say.

"Excuse me," the manager, a gray-haired black man, said. "Is there a problem? Might I be of some assistance? Maybe call the police?" He arched his eyebrows.

A crowd of curious onlookers began to congregate behind the manager. Brody stood there, sizing up the situation. He was a risk taker. He always talked about controversy. Controversy sold books.

And I'll be damned, I thought as I watched Brody's facial expression change. There it was, that look in his eyes. The last time I'd seen it, I was picking myself up off the floor after having all the wind knocked from my lungs. Hours later, I'd lost the baby.

"You alright?" a slender black waitress said.

Brody was seething; his half-closed eye was even smaller with anger. He looked like he wanted to cut loose but held his temper. He ran his hand over his cropped Afro, cracking a Colgate smile as if the camera hounds were popping off thousands of flashbulbs.

"Pumpkin, can we talk about this in the car?" he said calmly, stepping to me and gently grabbing my arm, the grip tightening with our every stride toward the door.

A murmur rose through the crowd.

"Ain't that the guy who wrote that novel?" a short, heavyset black woman asked. She was talking to a tall black man who looked like Tommy Ford from the *Martin* sitcom.

"And that's the co-author. Damn, we got two celebrities in the house," said a man sitting a couple tables over from the fat sista who'd made Brody.

Another powerful yank of my arm and I found myself being practically dragged out of the restaurant. Embarrassment was the last thing on my mind. I'd stopped being embarrassed after I'd turned my first trick. Shock registered on many of the black faces that made up a large percentage of the restaurant clientele. It really pissed me off to hear some of the ignorant sons of bitches laughing and applauding Brody's actions, like this was really an Ike Turner moment. But as swiftly as anger had come, it quickly gave way to sheer terror.

"Pregnant!" Brody yelled after we got home from the restaurant, pounding his fist on one of the glass end tables. He hit the table so hard that a picture of Michael Jordan fell from the wall. "Kimpa, I can't be no father right now. I'm not ready for the responsibility."

The handgun he pulled seemed to come from nowhere. It looked like one of those nine-millimeter things. He reached for me, but I managed to escape his grasp.

"Bring your ass here!" he screamed, stumbling over a duffel bag left on the floor.

"Are you crazy, Brody?" I asked.

Brody lunged at me again. My bob and weave eluded him. The only reason I could think of for his sudden rage was drug abuse. He had history, and it always repeated itself. The nigga had to be high, but how? I'd been with him all night, until the moment he'd gotten up from the table to take the phone call. He could've smoked crack in the bathroom or something.

His eyes were bloodshot red. My gaze never left the pistol in his hand. He staggered, falling over the arm of the sofa. I gasped for breath. Here I was, three months pregnant and running for my life. I almost twisted my ankle as I turned the corner, headed for the front door. Now I was silently cursing the house for being so huge. It was a symbol of our exodus from poverty. I wasn't about to let Brody turn it into a tomb. I remembered what I'd thought about at the restaurant, but all that mother grizzly bear noise went out the window because I was trying to get my unborn cub and me the hell out the house.

Finally reaching the door, I looked around to see where his crazy ass was. Safety was on the other side of the door. All I had to do was open it.

*Click*. I heard the ominous sound of a round being chambered into the barrel of the gun. Brody almost pulled my brain out of my skull when he yanked my ponytail. I fell backward, almost hitting the floor. Brody viciously yanked my ponytail again before I made contact. A sharp pain traveled across my hairline. Breathing heavily, Brody applied a police-style chokehold, bringing the barrel up to my temple.

I squirmed around inside his powerful grip until he roughly pressed the barrel to my jaw. I settled down right away.

"Scared, hunh?" the nigga asked, his hot breath scorching the fine hairs on my neck.

I shivered. I didn't know what to expect. He'd never pulled this tactic before.

"You've been real sassy lately. Getting real disrespectful. Not to mention I owe yo' ass for burning me. I don't know if you think I'm soft 'cause I got the best-selling book in the nation." He coughed. "It seems like you don't know your place anymore. And as the head of this relationship, I'm responsible for keeping you in your place."

He smacked me on the back of my head with the butt of the gun. I instantly saw bright lights. My legs tried to give way but Brody still had a good grip on my ponytail.

Why'd a bitch get rid of the scalpel? The damn thing would've come in handy at the present moment.

He violently shoved the gun into the small of my back. He was scaring the hell out of me. I couldn't see his face but his breathing was erratic. My mind traveled back to the day when I'd found Brody asleep and a crack pipe lying right next to him. I'd never said anything but it was happening again—book tours, talk shows, stress, crack.

"Baby, hunh?" he snorted, guiding me to the kitchen.

I said nothing. Just held my head and silently sobbed.

"You ain't slick. All of you hos are the same. Tryin' to drain all the life out of us men. That's why I ain't married you yet. I got too much money for somebody to be taking." He opened the door to the garage and shoved me in. I couldn't believe this arrogant son of a bitch had forgotten where he'd come from.

"Do you know how much money I'd have to pay out if you have a fuckin' baby? Next, you'll be tryin' to leave me." I didn't like the wild look in his eyes. I'd never seen it before. Never taking the gun off of me, Brody pushed the button, opening the garage door. Nighttime was in full bloom. Faint moonlight broke the void of darkness, separating the garage into light and shadows. A flimsy summer breeze drifted in. Our street was silent. My mind was on the gun, and Brody's intent. I wanted to fight but the muthafucka probably wouldn't hesitate to shoot.

I thought about all those cases where the husband or boyfriend had killed the wife or girlfriend and then disposed of the body. I thought about life on the street as a prostitute, about how a few of the girls I'd worked with had turned up missing, only to end up mutilated or shot in the head by some maniac and left in some abandoned building or field. Was I going to be one of those girls? Was this my fate? My mouth wouldn't let me say anything as

Brody pushed me in the direction of his newly acquired motor-cycle.

"The problem with you bitches is ya'll think ya'll are smarter than niggas. Ya'll think we just some kind of primitive cavemen. I love you but you'll never trap me with no baby."

He switched on the bike's ignition. The bright headlights sparkled into the darkness. Switching the gun to his left hand, Brody brought the bike to life. The Ninja roared with excitement. Cautiously, he put his helmet on, flipping up the visor. He motioned to another helmet on the back of the bike. "Put that shit on."

"Brody, I don't know about this," I whined.

"Put that shit on!" he yelled.

Now my mind had forgotten all about the threat of the gun and focused on the new threat. What the hell did Brody have up his sleeve? God only knew what he had in store. But a motor-cycle, alcohol, and madness weren't a good look.

"Get on," Brody said.

I hesitated a little until he waved the gun in my direction.

"Kimpa, get your ass on!" he said through angry, clenched teeth.

Brody tucked the gun back into his waistband, then I jumped on and held on tight. He flipped the helmet shield down. Brody hit first gear and we burned rubber out of the garage. I gripped Brody's body like I was a hungry anaconda. I didn't want to see where we were headed so I lowered my head, burying it securely in his back. All I could hear was the wind whistling as we passed car after car.

"Kimpa!" Brody yelled over the wind and the engine noise. "My question to you is will you get rid of the baby?"

He took my silence as a no and sped up. Brody started driving like a maniac, darting in and out of traffic at high speeds. It seemed

every sway of the bike drew horns from irate motorists. I understood his plan: to scare me into having an abortion. We zoomed
up one street and then down another. Where were the police
when you needed them? Brody cut loose with a hair-raising,
alcoholic war cry. With that, he gunned the bike.

"Kimpa, you can stop this if you just agree!"

I said nothing. I looked up just in time to see the headlights of
an oncoming eighteen-wheeler and heard the sound of urgency
in its horn.

Instinct caused me to slap Brody's helmet.

"Stop! Are you fucking mad? Brody, stop—stop!"

As the truck's horn grew louder and its headlights shone brighter,
I could hear a high-pitched scream.

Then, at the last minute, Brody hit the brakes, did some kind
of *Fall Guy* thing, and sped off in the other direction. I looked
back and watched in horror as the truck slid into a parked car,
demolishing it. I thanked God that no one was in the car. The
driver of the truck jumped out so he was all right.

Brody never stopped. To my surprise, I could hear his sinister
laughter as he glanced in the rearview mirror. I was sure that the
cops had a make on the bike by now. My heart was in my throat.
Brody had put us in the face of death and hadn't flinched.

I pleaded for him to stop. He slowed down enough to ask,
"Will you get rid of it now?"

I'd just about had enough.

"Anything, Brody!" I yelled. "Just let me off! Let me off!" I
pounded my fist against his back. "You, bastard, let me off!"

I was unaware but Brody was feeding off my fear. He gunned
the bike again, welching on his promise. It was hard to tell where
we were. The stretch of land we were on had no lampposts. We
were surrounded by complete darkness. But Brody obviously knew

where he was. The bike's headlights revealed clouds of dust. Brody slowed down to turn and for the next five minutes we bounced up and down on what appeared to be railroad tracks. Brody was trying his personal best to shake me up, or shake the baby out of me.

"B-B-B-Brody," I made an almost fruitless attempt to speak. "S-S-S-Stop!" My stomach was in knots. I felt queasy.

Brody growled and sped up. All I could do was hold on tight. Begging wasn't gonna stop him. At this point, nothing would.

This was *some* life. It was my body that had gotten us to this point. But now, I finally understood that it didn't mean anything. Brody had used me, letting me think that I was in control. He'd manipulated me, pulling my strings like I was a puppet. Typical man. I'd been conned. The worst part about it was that I'd brought this on myself. I thought I could play the game to get some cheese and ended up looking like a rat. I could feel tears slip down my cheeks.

The bike wobbled like it was out of control. It all felt like a dream. A nightmare. In the distance, I could hear someone screaming. Then amidst all the darkness, I blacked out.

M y vision was filled with fuzzy shapes and odd lights. I felt the presence of someone over me but I couldn't make them out. Whoever it was seemed to be gently rubbing my face. I tried to blink away the fog in my head but couldn't. The person seemed to be staring down at me as if in a deep trance, mumbling something. I couldn't make out the gibberish; didn't know if it was a prayer or some kind of a chant.

When the fog finally rolled away, I expected to see Saint Peter smiling at me but instead I saw Satan's sinister mug staring down at me like he was auditioning for a toothpaste commercial.

"I thought I lost you," Brody said, standing near my bed, stroking my cheek. The man standing next to Brody told the story. His nametag read *Yang*. My memory came back to me with fury: the motorcycle ride, the semi, and the frightening fall.

*The fall!* I yelled inside my mind. My eyes widened with fear. Instinctively I grabbed my stomach, looking from Brody's face back to the doctor's, then at my stomach.

"Sorry, Pumpkin," Brody spoke up. "The baby didn't make it."

I couldn't do anything but make little animal noises. I looked at the doctor for confirmation. He shook his head, giving me a look of condolence. Reality punched me in the teeth. I could remember so vividly now. Brody had been trying to scare me into having an abortion. That's when he took me to the railroad tracks, trying to shake the baby out of me.

"You and your husband were in a motorcycle accident, Ms. Peoples. I'm sorry you lost the baby."

Brody had planned the tracks, but not the fall. His selfish ass wouldn't put his own life and face in jeopardy. He was standing there looking at me like I better not say anything else, like if I opened my mouth to tell what he'd done, I would be sorry. That's when I noticed a huge white bandage that covered the right side of his head. I panicked. It didn't dawn on me that I might have been injured worse than Brody.

Fearfully, my right hand searched my head. My head was capped with a huge gauze bandage. The right side of my face was riddled with bumps and bruises. My bottom lip held six stitches. Then all at once, my body exploded into excruciating pain. My right arm was patched up. God only knew what kind of wounds lurked under the bandages. Tearfully, I tried to soothe my aching right arm with my left hand. To my surprise, I couldn't move it. My eyes swelled with tears. I tried everything in my power to move my left arm. I couldn't lift it. Had the fall paralyzed my left side?

Brody stood there, not saying a word, looking like he was

enjoying my little physical struggle. I had to calm myself down. I gave myself a few minutes while the doctor checked my vitals and bed chart. When I calmed myself, that's when I found out that I could lift my left leg. But when I removed the covers, I saw why I couldn't move my arm. My left arm had been placed in a cast. The white plaster covered my arm from my armpit down to my fingers.

The physical pain I was enduring paled in comparison to the mental agony. That's when it hit me: the life I'd had forming inside me had been terminated. Not by my choice.

"Oh my God!" I cried out in so much pain. "Not my baby!" Tears were sliding down my face, my mouth gaped open and long saliva-strands of anguish hung in the air like finally spawn spider-webs. I gently rubbed my stomach. "I'm sorry, baby, I was supposed to be there to protect you"—my chest heaved uncontrollably—"Brody, you bastard. You took another one from me! God, please forgive me—my baby, please forgive me."

I'd completely forgotten about Brody and the doctor standing over me. For the most part, I didn't give a damn.

"Fuck you, Brody!" I screamed. "You evil, self-centered sonofabitch! This shit was your fault!" I started snatching the IV from my arm and screaming like a cold, windy day. My hair was all over my head when I tried to jump out the bed and fuck Brody's bitch ass up.

"Pumpkin," Brody said straining, trying his best to restrain me, "what the hell are you doing?"

"Nurse, quickly," the little doctor called out, trying his hardest to control my kicking. After five minutes, one of the many nurses that rushed in at the doctor's call finally reestablished my IV. Working quickly, the fat black heifer gave me a dose of something that turned out the lights.

"It's a shame that Brody doesn't know how to treat a beautiful woman. I mean, dissing you like that in that restaurant. Now don't you want me to have my revenge? I'm sure your crumbling self-esteem would appreciate it." His creepy voice took on a condescending tone.

I was out of the hospital and at the crib. It'd been two weeks since the accident—although I wouldn't exactly call Brody's high-speed motorcycle, scare-tactic turned wipeout an accident. The spill had produced a broken left arm and a few healing abrasions. I now sported a long-armed cast stretching from my knuckles, stopping a few inches underneath my armpit. The thing itched like hell when my arm sweated.

And even though I'd been discharged two weeks ago from the hospital, my soul ached with the dry-rotting torment of a mother losing her baby. I'd been sitting in the family room, plotting how to pay his punk ass back with interest when the idea came in the form of a ringing telephone.

I knew who the threatening voice belonged to. It was the voice of the person Brody had crossed. I had forgotten about the shady character that had been making threatening phone calls and probably lurking around in the shadows. I'd forgotten about the real danger. I hushed and didn't say a thing; just tensed at the sound of his voice.

"Retribution is coming. If you don't believe me, perhaps you should take a look in your mailbox."

The phone went dead in my ear. I shivered at the silence that came afterward. My mind was running a mile a minute. My body went numb. The only thing I could feel was the pulsating pain beneath my cast. Quickly, I opened the bottle of pain pills and guzzled two of them with the help of spring water. I pulled my knees up to my chest and sat with my chin on them, looking at whatever creaked in the large room. Brody was gone away on some business and once again, I was all alone. Or was I?

I wanted to go to the mailbox but the darkness of night was holding me back. Brody had been in New York a whole week and the calls were frequent, coming almost every night since Brody had been gone.

Now I knew why I hadn't hipped Brody to the maniac: deep inside my soul I wanted Brody to pay with his life. This was the perfect opportunity. Fuck Brody! I wasn't telling him shit. But I didn't want to get caught up in the maniac's revenge game in the process. Brody was worth more to me alive than dead anyway. When I saw that his book career was blowing up, I immediately went out and secured a healthy life insurance policy on that bastard.

The way I saw it, I was going to get paid off his ass, one way or the other. I was snowbound past giving a fuck about him. I was only there because of the house. The bitch was part mine, too. We slept in separate bedrooms. The nigga better have been glad a bitch's left arm was in a cast. That was the only thing that kept me from wildin' on his ass whenever he slept—well, that and the West Bloomfield police. They weren't buying that shit. I'd gotten away with puttin' the smackdown on his bipolar ass in Detroit, but it wasn't gonna fly out there with those white folks. I had his bipolar, all right. If anything he was suffering from "crackpolar."

Curiosity led me to wonder what was in the mailbox. Call it stupid but I got up enough nerve to get my rump up off of the couch. Driven solely by fear and a yearning curiosity, I stuck my head out the family room door, surveying the hallway.

Nothing.

Slowly, I moved toward the door, my head moving back and forth like I was watching some kind of a tennis match. The long-armed cast I sported was extremely heavy and my arm itched like I had lice. The goon's threatening message replayed in my mind like a bad rerun. Cautiously, I made my way to the end of the hallway, one foot after another. I felt like I was in one of those horror movies where white folks always ended up dead, killed because of curiosity. But I had to see what was in the mailbox.

Before I opened the door, I went inside the coat closet and grabbed a Louisville slugger. It was like bringing a toothpick to a gunfight. I knew enough from all the movies I'd seen about gangstas that they carried semi-automatic weapons, guns that would make it hard for the victim to be identified by the next of kin.

One thing I hated about moving out into suburban Detroit was that all of the mailboxes sat out at the curb. Sure, it was convenient for the mail carrier, but an inconvenience for folks who had to take that long hike to fetch the mail; especially in hostile conditions.

Since I had a little flexibility in the hand of my injured arm, I cautiously opened the front door. My good hand clutched the bat. Even though the yard light revealed the dew on the grass, it still wasn't enough. I clicked on the porch light. Between the two, it seemed as if darkness stared in, afraid to come into the land of watts and volts. I opened the door and peeked around, readying my bat in a defensive posture. Not a soul was stirring.

At this point, I started missing the big city. On our old street, some people never went to sleep. There was always somebody outside. Right now I would've even welcomed the sight of Woody, the local bum in my old 'hood. As long as you gave him a bottle he would watch your property until the crack of dawn.

I stared out into the darkness and saw nothing moving. All I heard was the irritating sounds of crickets chirping. I looked in all directions. My mind raced with possibilities: would he try to use the darkness for cover while he relied on his sniper skills? Or would he be real and fight me face to face? As I drew closer to the mailbox, a twig snapped. My eyes bucked as I spun wildly in the direction of the sound.

"Who's there?" That was stupid, I thought as I tried to pull my heart out of my house shoes. I was sounding and acting more and more like the white folks in the scary movies. I stood there, poised in a striking position, looking like I was about to rip an imposing pitcher for a grand slam homerun.

I was guided by an overwhelming urge to see what Mister Big Time Writer had gotten himself involved in. Common sense grabbed hold of my emotions. The goon had put something in the mailbox that he wanted Brody to see. Therefore, I was acting as the messenger. The messenger always had immunity. I put a little bit more twist into my step, though I didn't relax completely. I'd done that once and Brody had ended up paying a ransom for me. As I opened my mailbox, my paranoia was replaced by a new kind of fear that came with the realization that this lunatic knew where we stayed, and had used this same handle to open my mailbox. I felt violated. Silly as it seemed, I felt that I was going to be blown to pieces when I opened the box. But something was inside; it was a legal-sized yellow envelope of some sort. I pulled it out and quickly darted back into the house.

I trembled all the way to the smallest bedroom in the house. Why the smallest bedroom? Because it gave me a sense of security. I looked around before putting my back against the wall. A pain sizzled through my cast while my good hand trembled as I slowly opened the envelope, the contents sliding back and forth as I angled the package.

The Polaroids I pulled out removed any doubts that I might have had about the threats made by my mysterious caller. I muffled a scream with the fingers protruding from my cast. My eyes were wider than silver dollars. The loud thumps of my heart could be heard in my ears, growing louder and beating faster at the grotesque sight of each picture. As I viewed the last Polaroid, my face froze in fear, my grip weakening and allowing the pictures to fall freely from my strong hand.

I couldn't move. Goosebumps walked the length of my arm. I stood there paralyzed by sheer terror. My knees buckled and down I went, falling right beside the pictures. Some were facedown, but the ones that had fallen face up caused my mind to reel with shock.

I was caught between worlds, fantasy and reality. That's it! I'd been dreaming a vicious nightmare filled with bloody dismembered bodies. Bodies with severed heads. The faces of young victims frozen in agonizing terror. Their eyes wide, caught in life's last surprising expression. But it was no dream. The photos were as real as the cast on my arm.

Slowly, I flipped over the facedown pictures. There was a strange familiarity about the men in the photos, like I'd seen them before. Where had I seen them? I thought about Brody, hoping that he wouldn't wind up on the next set of pictures to be mailed to me.

There was so much blood. The men were butchered like their lives had no meaning at all. Like they were cattle. What type of human being could kill and then take pictures like he'd created a masterpiece? The photos were mementos of madness frozen in time, a gory masterpiece telling the story of pain and suffering, ending eventually in death.

Story! Novel! That was it! Brody's novel. I willed myself to my feet. Somehow, I collected the pictures and was on my way to Brody's photo album, carefully glancing around for intruders. The novel, I thought again as I ran past the master bedroom right into Brody's office. Where had I seen these faces before? So much blood. Faces frozen. Dead. Butchered. The murderer had no fear of God. Maybe he thought he was a god.

Brody's bookcase sat at the back of his study. Thumbing my way past Richard Wright novels, Langston Hughes, Eric Jerome Dickey, dictionaries, reference guides, Literary Market Place, and right to the photo album, I flipped through until I found the matching faces. There they were. Brody and his childhood buddies. Their faces were much younger and filled with life, filled with humor. Brody stood in the middle, beaming like he hadn't a care in the world. Those happy days were long gone as I held up the photos of death. Three of the four were dead. Brody was the last one left. He'd sold out his friends. Broken the pact. Now, the dogs of war had been set loose. Something clicked in my mind. The first novel Brody had penned had been inspired by real-life events and now he was marked for death. And I feared for my safety because my dumb ass had put my name on as coauthor. I was scared, but I was no longer terrified. I had plans to leave Brody for good this time. And with any luck Brody would get bumped off after I was gone. The nigga put a gun up to my head. Fuck 'im. I wasn't showing him the pictures. I went and put 'em in the kitchen cabinet. To hell with his Forest Whitaker-looking ass.

"I got you, you sonofabitch!" I yelled, stomping through my hotel room four months later. I'd packed up and left Brody's punk ass before I caught a murder case. The Marriott was my temporary home. I'd come from the doctor's office, where I'd learned I was once again pregnant. I knew what that would mean when Brody found out. That's why he wasn't gonna find out. My baby would be months old before the fool had any idea. I wasn't trying to use my baby as a pawn but that nigga was gonna pay. All the money we'd made off the first book and I hadn't seen a dime of it. It was my fault; I'd gotten caught up in thinking a leopard could change its spots. Bad move. Because when I left Brody, he froze all the bank account and credit cards. But the joke was on him. I still had my CDs and the money I'd been squirreling away since I was on the streets. I knew how to survive. But that fool was going to pay. He would try to battle me for custody. It was about to get ugly so I had to get all my shit together. I had nine months to get my stuff in order.

It was hard to believe that I'd left that nigga four months ago. But I'd slipped up in a major way about a month earlier when I'd gone back to the house to retrieve the rest of my things. Brody and I had bumped uglies. I realized what I was doing. The lack of a condom made me vulnerable to STDs, but I'd gambled and come away healthy, holding the golden child. All the shit I'd gone through, I was entitled to half the estate. My whole campaign to grab security for myself had started with pimping myself out.

N ine months later, I welcomed the birth of a six-pound, chocolate-skinned baby boy. Brody Jr. was the name on his little ID bracelet. It was too early to say which one of us he favored. He was gorgeous, though.

Brody had found out about the baby when I ran up on him while I was out at the mall one day buying baby clothes. When I'd left home, I hadn't let him know my whereabouts. Kept playing the old hotel shell game on his ass. I didn't wanna see 'im until the baby and I were ready to take his ass to court for our share of that loot he was sitting on. But when he'd seen me at the mall with my belly hanging out, I let him know. I was a good seven months along by then and he wasn't stupid. Hitting me in the stomach would've been seriously bad for his career. Mister Big Time Writer's next composition would be written from the state penitentiary while washing the drawers of his cellmate.

To my surprise, Brody was genuinely happy. The nigga seemed to have had a change of heart. He wanted me to move back in. When I rejected his offer, he went and bought me a condo. I didn't reject that offer. Just laid down some rules. He was kissing my ass now and I loved it, but I wasn't gonna drop my guard. There was no telling what he had up his sleeve. Having his baby gave me power, and Brody's controlling ass didn't like it. So I had to keep my wits about me. Brody was dangerous and out of his mind. He was also a master of manipulation. All it took for me to end up his victim again was for me to fall for the okey-doke.

I had been cooped up in the house since I brought my son home from the hospital. Brody hired Mrs. Lenny to sit with the baby at his house whenever it was his weekend to spend time with Lil' Brody. The baby was four months now and it was Brody's weekend to keep him while I got out to enjoy a little me-time.

I was out shopping when I stumbled upon an old familiar face. It'd been a couple years and the face before me held a few wrinkles and sagging skin, but other than that, Stanley Larkin looked great. I was checking out the latest CDs when I bumped into him.

He was so surprised to see me that he gave me a great big bear hug, generating some attention inside the shopping store. Being that Stan was white, the brothers stared insanely at our reunion, and the white folks turned up their noses in disgust. But none of that mattered. Stan was a sight for sore eyes. We talked for about twenty minutes in the store, then we went and had lunch at Olga's. We talked about new and old times, joking and laughing about me being a mom when it seemed like just yesterday I was a baby myself.

"Stan, I'm not a baby anymore. I'm twenty years young."

Stan smiled. "A whole twenty, hunh? But, my dear, you look stunning at twenty."

He told me that he'd finally left his wife and had sole custody of his two teenage sons. Said he was still practicing law and if I ever needed him to give him a call. He handed me his business card, we hugged, and after that we parted company.

Twenty minutes later, I was pulling up in the driveway of Brody's house. Dusk had settled and the house was unusually silent. A chill grabbed my body. Something wasn't right and I felt it. I still had a key so I let myself in. A coppery smell saturated the air. I couldn't quite place it.

I thanked God that I was no longer hindered by that stupid cast. I moved through the hallways slowly. Creeping through the shadows of this big house reminded me of the night I'd crept outside and retrieved those pictures. This was becoming a regular house of horrors. Almost every place I looked brought back a horrible memory. If I won the house in a lawsuit, I would sell it. I couldn't raise my baby in the creepy crib.

I was upstairs now and peering into Brody's study. He must've been gone 'cause his door was wide open. My thoughts quickly went to Mrs. Lenny, the nanny, and my baby. Where were they?

Quickly but quietly I moved back down the stairs. This was crazy. Something wasn't right and here I was playing detective. What if there had been foul play? My chest tightened and my stomach tumbled with nervous energy. I cursed myself for leaving my infant with a defenseless old woman, knowing that there was a killer stalking Brody.

The house was far too big for me to search for clues. As I moved through the darkness, my mind recalled so many of the threatening messages I'd heard from the maniac. Where was my child? My heart was beating super fast. I wanted to cry and scream. Coming down the spiral staircase I could hear a slight moaning emanating from the kitchen. With cautious steps, I inched my way toward the noise. My baby—where the hell is he? The need to find my child pushed me through the dark recesses of the house.

The moaning was getting louder as I approached the kitchen. This was the darkest part of the house. At this point, I had to think real hard. There was a fucked-up chance of me catching a bullet if I turned on the kitchen light. The thought marinated in my mind for a few seconds. Anxiety burned in my chest. Flipping on the lights and having my lights flipped off at the same time scared the ghost out of me. But I had to find my baby. I flipped the kitchen light on.

When the lights came on, I kind of wished that I'd left them off. The coppery smell I'd noticed back when I first entered the house was blood—which was all over the marble tile, pooled in puddles streaming from beneath the broom closet door.

Not fearing anything, I rushed over and opened it. I was both relieved and scared at the same time. Mrs. Lenny's body lay curled up in the fetal position. I checked her pulse.

Nothing.

Guess she must've moaned her last breath out before I'd opened the door. I didn't have to roll her over to see the large bullet hole through her back. The burned, jagged edges of black skin almost made me throw up and I did, all over the floor. I was hunched over, almost on my knees, when I felt a sharp pain cut across my left shoulder blade. Blackness.

"Wake up, sleepyhead," a deep voice said softly from outside the fog. The dizziness was lifting but my head throbbed. I sluggishly tilted my head to one side. "You're even more beautiful up close. Binoculars don't do you no justice. Not at all."

My eyes were blurry at first. Blurry, blurry, blurry—then I focused. I knew who he was right away. His face was even scarier than his voice. Horrifying. But there he stood, as creepy as ever. At an astonishing six-foot-four, he was meaty around the shoulders, with a neck like Mike Tyson. The right side of the man's face looked normal, but his most terrifying feature was his left, which looked like it had been doused with acid. The man looked like a badly burned corpse. No left eyebrow or eyelashes. *No eyebrow?* I thought.

It was the man from the restaurant! A whole year's worth of fear washed over me, and a single tear slowly dripped down my cheek, followed by a steady stream.

Almost instantly I discovered that my arms and legs were bound to a heavy armchair. I struggled but the phone cord he'd used to tie me up with cut into my wrists and ankles. My eyes widened with fear as I tried to speak.

He seemed to enjoy my fear. "I told you that I would be about my business." He put his hand up to his lips. "I know you didn't think I forgot about that piece of shit. Here I am! Come to collect on my threat." He looked down at himself. "The devil in the flesh."

Like that of all bad men, his body was draped in crow-black garments. My eyes never left the big, chrome gun in his right hand. I sat in the den overlooking the patio. The sliding doors were directly across from me. This was the first time I thought about Brody.

"Why did you have to hurt the old woman and where's my baby?" I finally got enough nerve to ask, fearing the answer.

He arrogantly scratched his forehead with the barrel. "Brody left an hour ago. Expecting 'im back soon. Real soon," he said, evading my questions.

I could only assume the worst. I tearfully nodded in the direction of the body.

"Why?" I questioned with tears slipping silently from my eyes.

He chuckled nonchalantly, smiling devilishly. I didn't know what was more frightening—his low, morbid voice or his burned-up kisser.

He surveyed our house.

"I swear. That nigga got all this" —he waved his hands around my lavishly furnished former home—"just from telling my story. I made ya'll rich simply by puttin' caps in niggas." He arched his bushy eyebrows sheepishly. "Feel like I should be cut in. After all, it's just bidness. But back to your question, I'm a sick, twisted, tormented human being. I asked him for one simple thing and he lied to me…flat-out lied. I swear, I don't know what I hate the most, liars or thieves."

He gestured with the gun, pointing it in the direction of the closet where Mrs. Lenny lay. "Brody's going to die because he saw too much, plus he couldn't keep his mouth closed. I'll shut it permanently. When that story-stealing mothafucka gets back, I'm going to kill you all." His eyes held a hellish threat. Just then my baby let out a stifled cry. My breath caught in my throat and my heart skipped beats. My eyes roamed wildly around the room, trying to locate which door the sound had escaped from.

"Don't worry, he's still alive…for now. Aww, don't cry, pretty. It'll all be over soon enough."

I was silently praying with my eyes open when I witnessed a wonderful miracle. While the killer had his back turned toward the patio door, I could see the knob moving as if God Himself was coming in to punish this man for all his wrongdoing. I had to distract the killer, and quickly.

"Can I have a glass of water?" I asked, straightening my face. He looked at me suspiciously, then walked to the kitchen. Oh my God, I silently screamed. Brody was walking into a hit fresh from the pages of his bestseller. I had to think quickly.

Brody slid the patio door back and strolled in like he didn't have a freakin' care in the world. Judging from his bloodshot eyes, it was safe to say that the fool had been sucking on a bottle of alcohol. He spotted me, and a look of confusion washed over his face. The next look the bum gave me suggested that he thought I was playing some kind of sexual bondage game with myself.

"Brody, shhh," I whispered. "He's in the kitchen. Untie me. We have to find the baby."

Just as Brody finally pulled my restraints loose, we were surprised by the creep, holding a glass of water. Without word or warning, Brody bum-rushed the psycho, who threw down the glass and, with inhuman speed, drew a pistol the size of a small hand cannon from his waistband and took aim.

Brody slammed into the hit man with a force strong enough to knock the pistol loose. It fell, striking the tile floor and discharging. The blast was super loud, like a bazooka going off. The shot took out the patio glass, shattering it into millions of tiny pieces.

Brody and the manic wrestled for control. The killer landed a sharp uppercut to Brody's jaw and Brody hit the floor as if the blow had shattered his bones into itty-bitty pieces.

I'd been frozen with fear all that time, and I finally thawed long enough to dash for the pistol on the floor, but caught a boot to the back for my efforts. The hit man picked up the pistol. But Brody wasn't done. He sprang from the floor and tried to attack the hit man again. When the cannon went off this time the force from the impact slammed Brody's body against the wall. He slid down the wall, a blood trail following. I couldn't tell where he'd been shot. The blood splatter on the wall with the bullet hole going through it told me that the bullet had traveled straight through. I didn't know if Brody was dead or not.

"Now, I finish you," he said to me, once again taking a two-handed aim. It was exactly like they say: I saw my life pass before my eyes. Saw Momma in a white gown; saw my baby with his newly adopted parents, passed around from foster family to foster family as if he was a wine bottle in a circle of winos. I broke and ran through the doorway leading to the living room and up the stairs as quickly as I could, horrified of what could've become of my baby, all the while expecting to hear the gun go off again.

I slammed and locked the door of the master bedroom, rifling through the chest of drawers for the pistol Brody had put away. Searching inside the walk-in closet, I almost jumped out of my skin when the cannon roared again. And even though I didn't see it, I could tell the door had been completely blasted into splinters.

"Bitch, now you join Brody." Standing at the door of the closet, the killer aimed the gun at my face.

"Freeze," I heard someone command from behind. The maniac turned around ready to shoot, but received a slug in the leg and one in the chest. Police stormed through the bedroom doorway like storm troopers. What can I say? Living in the suburbs meant you belonged to a block association. The shots were so loud that one of the neighbors heard them and had immediately called 9-1-1.

"My baby!" I shouted at one of the officers. "The sonofabitch took my baby!"

I muscled my way through the sea of blue uniforms to the hallway where my motherly hearing picked up muffled cries coming from the guest bedroom off the stairs. I rushed in, the cries leading me in the direction of the closet. I swung the door open so hard, I almost tore it off the hinges. Lil' Brody was lying on the floor. His face was soaked with tears but he was otherwise no worse for wear. I picked my precious up and soothed him with kisses.

Mister Big Time Writer survived with a shoulder wound, as did the killer. After weeks of questioning, the killer finally broke down and confessed to numerous unsolved murders.

Further police investigation uncovered the truth behind the killer's bloody rampage. Brody told the police investigators—and his story was also verified by the killer—it happened when Brody and his friends were teens, playing one evening in a wooded area. When they'd come across five men holding automatic rifles, dressed in black jumpsuits with Mafia Incorporated stitched on their backs in big yellow letters, standing in front of three men on their knees, hands crossed behind their heads. Brody informed them that the men on their knees ranged in age, one younger man and two older, both with thick beards. Brody and his friends had hunched down out of sight behind some brush with a clear view of the scene. One of the men in black had stood out from the rest, a little taller, but had done all the talking. The taller man went on to explain that the men kneeing the earth where rival drug lords who were charged with trying to expand their operations inside of Mafia Incorporated territory.

When the bullets started to fly, Brody and his buddies tried to sneak away, but were spotted by a sixth Mafia member, probably a lookout, and marched at gunpoint to where the bloody bodies lay. Brody said since they were kids, the leader gave them a break, and in exchange for their silence about the executions, they were released, but with a warning. They would be hunted down and executed if they ever mumbled a peep. Brody had broken the covenant by publishing Mafia Incorporated's dirty laundry, almost like snitching in print. Mafia Incorporated had taken exception and released the hound of hell in the form of the grossly disfigured, psychotic killer. Brody's friends were mercilessly butchered for the glory of his own selfish pursuit of literary greatness.

Brody blamed me for everything and filed for sole custody of Lil' Brody. In court, he brought up every sin I'd ever committed. Brody played up the whole prostitute angle, branding me as an unfit mother.

To sell it, Brody's bipolar ass had even managed a few tears. Brody also provided pictures of Stanley and me hugging. I found out that he'd been having me followed by some private investigator since the birth of the baby. After Brody's high-powered attorney got through with me, he made me look like I was unfit to own a dog.

Brody's money was long and it allowed him to produce some of my former tricks, and other working women like Sensation, whom I'd considered family. Seeing her appear on Brody's list of witnesses rocked me to the core. The skank had sold me up the river, trading whatever integrity she had left for an undisclosed amount of loot. I should've drowned that ho when I had a chance during our few trips to relax in the whirlpool. Naturally Brody added the accounts of a few pimps and storeowners to make his unfit mother strategy stick. I was done for. Brody and I weren't married so I wasn't entitled to a damn thing. The court awarded Brody full custody. All of that, and I don't think his intentions for little Brody were even sincere. The ink hadn't dried on the judgment when Brody hired movers to set my shit out on the streets.

"So, America," I spoke tearfully into the microphone, "There you have it. We, as women, have to stand up to the self-proclaimed 'superior gender.' We have to stand united in the fold of sisterhood and vow to never put a man ahead of our self-esteem. Let my story serve as a cautionary tale against it."

Tears cascaded down my cheeks. I wiped them away with the sleeve of my sweater. Mindspeak had a look of horror on his face. I could see inside the sound room. Donna was sobbing into a tissue. Isis was nodding her head in approval. The pain from the Old Lady was tearing me a new one.

Isis and Donna trotted into the room. Mindspeak instantly perked up.

"It's time for me to do my thing," Isis said, her gun fixed on Mindspeak.

"Before you do," I said, cringing from the pain, "Isis, I have to go to the ladies room."

"Kimpa, can't it wait?" she asked with that hard look on her face.

The dozens of painful wrinkles in my face answered.

"That time of the month, hunh?" Donna asked with a look on her face that said she was glad it wasn't her. "Sweetie, the bathroom is out that door and to the left. Do you have everything you need? Maybe you better go to my personal bathroom. It's out the hallway, first door to the right. You'll find everything you need."

A simple nod of my head and I stepped off in the direction of Donna's bathroom.

I came back refreshed but the pains were hitting me in the stomach as if I was suffering from severe gas and acute food poisoning, all while being punched in the gut repeatedly by Mike Tyson.

"You ready, girl?" Isis asked, looking eager to make it do what it do.

I nodded my head. I admit to being angry, too, but her kind of rage was silent, explosive. She'd never fully told me her story, only snippets. Even though the heifer had the body of a woman, her ordeal had left her with a coldness uncharacteristic for her gender, totally desensitized to emotions and feeling. Although I was scared out of my mind with visions of being gunned down by the police, I couldn't wait to hear her story. I needed to understand everything that she had been through and since we were already there, and I had already taken a turn on the microphone to tell the world everything, she deserved that opportunity as well. After all, the entire hostage scenario was her idea.

Donna and I went to the sound room. While Donna probably assumed my uncontrollable trembling was from the pain of the cramps, I was really sobbing for the baby that I would never get to see again—well, except on visiting days if Brody softened up and grew a heart.

Isis smiled at me, giving me the thumbs-up sign as she slipped on the headset. She was getting settled in when the phone in the corner rang.

"That's our direct number," Donna said.

"What does that mean?" I wanted to know. I held the gun down at my side. I wanted to drop it. The lady seemed nice enough and she didn't deserve what was happening.

"The line is private. Family and other VIPs use it."

"Answer it," I said. I was warming to Donna. The photos on her corner desk displayed the smiling faces of her little growing babies. She was a mother and so was I. I wasn't gonna hold the pistol on her and risk having the gun accidentally discharge, ripping a mother away from her children.

Donna picked up the phone. Isis threw her hand in the air, wanting to know what the holdup was. I waved my finger in the air, signaling her to chill for a minute.

Donna had this dumbfounded look on her face as she handed me the phone.

"It's the police," she said. "They want to talk to you."

I took the phone. "Yeah," I answered. I listened, then gestured for Isis to come into the room.

Isis came in, still holding the gun on Mindspeak as he marched in front of her.

"What's the holdup this time?" she wanted to know.

"It's the police," I explained. "They want to talk to you."

Shaking like a leaf on a tree, I politely handed her the phone. I wasn't built for this shit. This was not something I could handle.

"Yes," Isis said in a no-nonsense voice as she listened for a second. "We won't negotiate. The only negotiation we'll consider comes *after* we've finished on the air. Only then will we listen, but for now, don't send in a soul. We've got all the entrances covered," Isis explained, acting like she'd done this before. She hung up.

"Kimpa, please don't fall to pieces on me now," Isis begged. "We're halfway there."

Isis marched Mindspeak back into the studio.

I was worried, scared. The idea of being shot for the cause didn't sound appealing. But I did what she asked and soon Donna was counting down.

"Four...three...two...one."

"America, my name is Isis." I could hear her voice in the sound room. "This is my story."

"Isis, I just want you to get serious about your life," my auntie Ruthie Jean Sampson said in a voice tailored by old age. "Jim and I aren't trying to keep you from having your fun at the clubs and hanging out with friends. We're worried about your future. We're not going to be around forever and we want you to have some security."

My uncle Jim butted in. "Isis…" he said, then stopped to breathe deeply into the mask that was connected to a portable oxygen tank. "These streets are dangerous and are no place"—he took a deeper drag on oxygen—"no place for a young lady. You can do anything you want. We're behind you. Just slow down. We see tragedy on the news every day."

When were they gonna get off my case? I'm sure they were allowed to have fun when they were kids, centuries ago. I'd just graduated high school and here they were trying to discourage me from having a little fun.

Why couldn't I be left alone? I was eighteen and, like many young women brimming with youth, I was out of school for the summer and ready to enjoy all the simple pleasures of being young and gifted with the devastatingly curvaceous body of an ebony goddess.

Now here they were trying desperately to kill my buzz, stopping me from hanging with my girls, tearing up the shopping malls and flaunting our sexy young bodies in the clubs while men tripped all over themselves trying to get us to give them the time of day. It was just a good time. Nobody was getting hurt.

For Christ's sake, I'd been given an academic scholarship to attend the University of Michigan, majoring in elementary education. But that didn't seem to matter to those two; they tirelessly rode my back, always preaching sermons about how they'd lived when racism was still legal. I wasn't gonna let them ruin my last moments of freedom before I fully committed myself to a future in teaching.

I was young and eager to experiment with life. I loved our culture and its people. I immersed myself in its richness with both feet and could find some good in even the worst and lowest forms of humanity. Most of my girlfriends joked that I was a nerd trapped inside the body of a stripper. My education had all to do with me not speaking hood dialect. It wouldn't flow right from my tongue. So I was often ridiculed for my pronunciation of some slang words.

I sat on a much worn, floral-printed couch, listening to them with my head, but not taking their obsessive concerns to heart. What did they know? I mused while examining how Father Time was smacking the both of them around like they were WWE superstars in a serious cage match. Auntie Ruthie's once long and lustrous black head of hair had been traded in for a cropped gray bob. She couldn't walk without the assistance of a cane, and Uncle Jim couldn't leave the house unless he was accompanied by his oxygen tank. Uncle Jim used to be a very handsome, tall drink of water, but old age had diminished his height, slightly stooping him over at the waist and slowing his once proud peacock-like strut into a clumsy foot shuffle, helped along by a walker.

Their constant nagging had been playing in my ear like an old blues song all those years. They were totally detached from my generation, without a clue about what made us tick. My mother and father—God bless their souls—had been taken away from me in a car accident when I was five. The story that I had gotten was that some idiot had come out of nowhere, running the light and smashing into them, T-boning their car. When the police and ambulance arrived, my folks were dead, but somehow the driver responsible had managed to free himself from his twisted wreckage and flee the scene.

I stood from the couch, brushing away the wrinkles in my black skirt. It was Saturday night and I wasn't about to waste it hanging around with my aunt and uncle. I loved them beyond the grave, but I had to experiment with life.

The absence of both parents presented challenges and raised questions about my identity; I never really understood much about them since I was so young. I would've liked to have gotten to know them. But for the most part, I tried to draw strength from realizing that I was growing into a strong black woman who'd persevered by powering through the pitfalls offered up by a hostile environment.

The last thing I heard my Aunt Ruthie Jean say to me when I left for the club that night was, "Isis, be careful out there."

I wish that I would've listened. My aunt and uncle had done a great job of raising me. They had seen things in me that I didn't see in myself. I understood correctly that I was one of those souls who trusted others to the point of being gullible. And sometimes that's more dangerous than being paranoid. Some of my girl-friends might've called me intelligent but, in the same breath, behind my back, they'd say that I lacked street smarts. I never argued the point because it was true.

If I had street smarts, I would've never let Denairo Ganteeny buy me a drink at Rock Bottoms. I was underage, but sometimes the bartender at the club would slip us something for a monetary incentive. Denairo Ganteeny slid the bartender a twenty.

"The name's Denairo—Denairo Ganteeny," he said smoothly, extending his hand to me and smiling with a mouthful of pretty pearly whites.

He was so fine, I had to open and close my eyes to see if he was actually real. Denairo's pretty, black, curly hair and deep rich dimples highlighted his fabulous chestnut complexion. He had to be mixed race, Black and Italian probably. There was no other way to explain his freakish good looks. The club had a relaxed dress code so he was wearing a nice black and white button-down, black slacks, and some bangin' shoes—which were new, by the way.

"I'm sorry," I said, blushing, taking the glass of wine from the bartender. I sipped some, shaking his hand. "My name is Isis. It's a pleasure to meet you."

"Isis…that's it, no last name?

"Just Isis."

His voice was a firm, strong baritone that made me quake with desire every time he spoke. I wanted him to keep talking so that I could secretly live out my fantasy of us on a deserted island somewhere in the Pacific.

"Well, *Just Isis*, you and your name are both gorgeous. You remind me of Alicia Keys." He examined me from head to toe. "Signature Cache top, capri pants, and sexy peek-a-boo heels. You have exquisite taste in clothing."

He had me blushing like a sixth-grade girl receiving her very first kiss.

"Thank you. You are very handsome yourself," I returned the compliment.

My girl, Tisha, wiggly walked her long, slender body off of the dance floor. Tisha was so drunk that she was bumping into people trying to get their groove on. The place was packed in tight with no allowance for personal space.

As the music blared in the background, Tisha, reeking of booze and bad breath, sat on the barstool next to me. I was really into clothes but what Tisha was wearing all but defied description or explanation. She was my girl and everything, but the heifer was one bad outfit away from a life sentence inside a penitentiary for the fashionably illiterate. Like tonight, Tisha was prancing around in some baby doll shoes, leggings and a pink shirt featuring the face of Bozo the clown that looked like she'd made a personal trip back to the seventies in a time machine to make her purchases.

She leaned on my shoulder, drenched with perspiration, swinging her phony ponytail, taking my drink from my hand and draining it. Tisha's eyes were small and glazed over. Her bangs lazily drooped across her forehead and her hair was matted to her head by oceans of sweat.

"Who you?" she asked Denairo, leaning across my body like she was going for a kiss.

I thought I would die from embarrassment. Tisha was the alcoholic of our clique. She never bought any drinks herself but had great mooching skills when it came to finishing the ones that would be sitting on the table in front of us.

Denairo smiled that amazing smile and reached over me to shake Tisha's hand.

"I'm Denairo Ganteeny, the man responsible for the last bit of alcohol you consumed."

Tisha never shook his hand, just stared at it like it was covered in dog mess. Then she sluggishly stared him in the face.

"Well, Al Pacino, you can buy her another one. You look like you a baller." She laughed so hard, she almost launched herself from the barstool.

Lisa arrived just in time to run "Operation Babysitter." Tisha was always out of control when she had liquor in her system and Lisa was the only one who could do anything with her when she started tripping. So Lisa would operate as Tisha's official chaperone.

"Hey, Tisha." Lisa walked up behind her, dressed in slacks and a nice top we'd picked up from Macy's for a steal. "I think I locked my keys in my car. Come help me."

"Where's your manners?" Tisha asked, her voice fuzzy with alcohol. "Can't you see I'm talking with Al Pacino here? What I look like anyway? A slim-jim to you?"

Lisa pulled Tisha from the barstool. She'd run damage control before so she knew how to handle Tisha's when she was really drunk. "Tisha, a little more action from the hips and a little less lip, please."

"No. I want to stay and kick it with Scarface," Tisha protested as Lisa pulled her away. "Hey, Al, say hello to *my* little friend. Where's your boy, Manny Ribera, and why you smoke him at the end? Did you really wanna bone your sister?" she yelled over her shoulder.

"Well, I'm extremely embarrassed now," I said, wanting to shrink into a microscopic organism. The people around us were in stitches as Lisa dragged Tisha away.

Al—I mean Denairo—brandished that pretty smile. I melted.

"She's alright. Pretty entertaining, if you ask me." He ordered me another drink. "I get that Scarface thing all the time. After a while you sort of get used to it, I guess."

We sat there talking for a few hours. I was buzzed and feeling good. He was so easy to talk to and it seemed like I could tell him anything.

Matter of fact, I was so buzzed that I later found myself on the flat roof of an old apartment building, gazing through some high-powered binoculars, observing a middle-aged black man. The man looked mighty familiar. I couldn't place him.

I'd left the club with my girls. After they dropped me off at home, I pretended to go in the house but shot around back and ran up the alley to meet Denairo three streets over. I knew my girls, especially Lisa, would try to talk me out of going, so I hadn't filled them in on my plans. We drove around until about six, laughing and talking. At one point, he let it be known that he was an FBI agent, flashing his credentials and everything. I had to be buzzing when I let him convince me to go up on this building to do surveillance.

But there he was, kneeling right next to me as the sun started to make its way up, turning the sky golden and announcing a brand-new day.

The man that I was peering at looked like an ordinary elderly man, about five-foot-six, with a small frame and a peanut head. The old man gazed around like he was suspicious of something.

Denairo disappeared for a moment while I kept looking. He returned, kneeling again, but this time he was clutching a high-powered rifle.

My heart jumped into my throat.

"What are you—"

He shushed me. I shook nervously, trying to focus on the man, who was now making his way to his Ford Taurus.

I couldn't imagine what this poor man had gotten himself into, but before I could think about it further, Denairo pulled the trigger. No noise. The silencer on the end of the barrel sup-pressed any sound.

Through the binoculars, I saw the black man disappear behind a curtain of his own blood. He was thrown against the passenger side of the vehicle by the impact, sliding down the door and leav-ing blood streaks.

I almost screamed but I muffled my mouth. Tears slowly slid down my cheeks. Through the glasses the blood looked dark, almost black. Denairo had done his homework well. At this hour, nobody was out. The streets were desolate. The man's body had come to rest on the ground, sitting spread eagle with his head and back resting against the car door. I dropped the binoculars after glancing upward at the car windows. I looked at Denairo.

The way he was cheesing, I thought I was being punked. I kept looking around to see if the camera crew was going to come rushing out. I peeked through the binoculars again to see if the man was now standing up, waving at me and wiping away fake blood with a crowd of people around chuckling insanely at my expense. But the man was definitely not laughing or moving. His brains were splattered everywhere.

Without warning, I vomited. Denairo looked at me and laughed. In no time, he had the rifle broken down and back in the briefcase. We were off of the roof and back in the car in a flash. I was crying. Shaking. Babbling. Trying to make sense of what had happened and wondering how one minute I was enjoying a pleasant conversation with a great guy and the next I was witnessing a homicide.

"Oh my God," I said, ruining my mascara with tears that I couldn't seem to stop. "You just killed him. You killed that man. You killed him. *Oh my God, you killed that man!*" I screamed over and over.

Before he drove off, he shoved a small pistol in my face. His eyes were deadly slits, his face a silent portrait of insanity. I didn't know this man at all. He wasn't the one I'd met at the bar. My grandparents were right; I was too trusting and now I was certain to end up like that man back there.

"Let me make your acquaintance again. My name is Denairo Ganteeny and I kill people for a living." He pointed in the direction of the dead man. "Welcome to my world. The only way out is death. If you want out"—he pressed the gun to the side of my temple, cocking it—"I'll have to kill you."

I shivered, nodding in submission.

"Good. I would hate to have to kill such a beautiful woman."

The smile was back but it wasn't so amazing anymore. I couldn't look at him. His eyes twinkled like those of a vampire before sinking his fangs into his victim's neck. He was a monster, an animal with no regard for human life. I had been blindsided by his charismatic demeanor and charming sense of humor. I was cold and shivering in the presence of a cold-blooded killer.

He put away the weapon and we drove away just in time. A blur of flashing beacons and wailing sirens flew by us at high speed. We didn't talk. I didn't know what lay ahead of us. All I knew was my life would never be the same. I was instantly a prisoner. With one bullet, he'd introduced me to his world of death by contract killing.

I cried as Denairo drove the little Ford Focus until the buildings, gas stations, corner liquor stores, the sights and sounds of the big city were replaced by open roads, five-lane highways with truck stops every few miles, and cows and horses grazing in enormous green pastures.

In my mind, I made several attempts to break and run, but in each scenario, I ended up with my brains all over the sidewalk.

"My aunt and uncle are worried sick right now," I said to Denairo as he pulled off the interstate and into a wooded area. "Please let me go. I promise that I won't tell anybody. It'll be our secret."

But he looked at me and flashed that demented smile again, getting out of the car. He was going to kill me. This area was ideal for dumping a body. It was uninhabited by anything other than wildlife.

When he went into the trunk, I made my move, opening the door, trying to sprint in my heels. I got a solid three feet away before going down, a hole in the grass snagging my left heel. I hit the grassy dirt with a thud, almost knocking myself senseless.

Through the dust that surrounded my body, I could see Denairo walking toward me with rope in one hand and duct tape in the other.

"Gopher holes out here, honey. It seems you're wearing the wrong running shoes."

The next thing I knew, I lay cramped in the backseat underneath a comforter, gagged with duct tape and with my hands and feet tied like a sow on my way to the slaughterhouse. I was crying so hard, I gave myself a headache.

I could only guess that we'd been on the road for roughly five or six hours. I was pissed and frightened even more than I'd been when I thought Wilber Charles had gotten me knocked up after we had gotten it on backstage at an eighth-grade dance. My poor aunt and uncle. They had to be sick with worry. By now they had called Tisha and Lisa to inquire about me. Over the years they'd grown hip to our schemes and the way we covered for each other. I took a little comfort in knowing that Tisha and Lisa had seen Denairo and could describe him to the police. The cops were probably on our trail right now.

"Listen, Isis," Denairo said, turning the radio down a little from the news broadcast. "I don't want to harm you. Do what I say and we'll get along just fine. Disobey me and we'll have issues that'll produce consequences. Now, I'm only going to tell you this one time, so listen up. Trying to run on me again can be bad for the lives of—what're their names again? Yes, I remember now—Tisha, Lisa, and her new boyfriend, not to mention your aunt and uncle."

He paused for a moment to give his threats a chance to sink in, and when they did, goose bumps marched up my entire body and I cried tears the size of hailstones. This man had just gotten creepier.

"I'm Al Pacino, remember? I would hate to have to go over Tisha's house and show her *my* little friend." He paused for another creepier-than-thou moment. "It was a joke, my little Alicia Keys look-alike, but I would kill her though, just so you know. You play by my rules and you have no reason to fear for the safety of your loved ones." He paused one last time, then dropped a nuclear bomb. "Oh, yeah, you can never go home again."

The impact of his statement caused me to thrash around on the backseat, hoping and praying that some trucker would notice and alert the state police. I continued until I was a sobbing mess of tears, perspiration, and snot. I can't tell you what happened next because I blacked out.

When I came to, I had lost all track of time. It was so dark, I couldn't see my hand in front of my face. I wiggled around but I was still tied up. I didn't know if he had stuffed me in the trunk or what. I cried, thinking about all of the people that I would never see again. I didn't know why he was doing this to me. All I had tried to do was enjoy myself before I went off to college. All that seemed like a dream or some faraway and distant memory now. I had no idea what this man was going to do to me.

My poor Auntie Ruthie Jean had to be having a fit. My girls were no doubt beside themselves with grief. If this had happened to one of them, I would've been going out of my mind trying to find her. Tisha, Lisa, and I were like the Three Musketeers. We'd had each other's backs since first grade. And I was paying the ultimate price for not adhering to the Three Musketeers' dating rules. The most serious rule a woman could ever break was, "Never let your girl go home with a strange man, no matter how charming he pretends to be or how much money he's flashing around." I was even guiltier because I'd never given Lisa and Tisha a chance to stop me.

I hadn't been much of a devout church member. I only attended when Auntie Ruthie would throw a tantrum and force me to go. But other than that, Sunday was about breakfast, lunch, and mall-hopping with the girls. Despite my less than stellar church attendance record, I'd never lost track of my praise for the Lord. I was a good girl who possessed a healthy love of human life. Why was God letting this happen to me?

The door that opened just then wasn't really much of an answer from the Lord but I'd never been so glad to see daylight. It flooded the little windowless room that held me captive. The glare from the light was blinding. I could make out Denairo as he walked in, holding a knife. My heart jumped into my mouth. I was lying on the floor in the corner. If he was going to do it, I wished he'd get it over with. The anticipation was killing me.

He knelt down beside me, cutting through my ropes. I jumped at the sound of steel meeting rope as it made that cutting noise.

"Listen, I'm going to take this tape off. Don't scream. Scream and it goes right back on. I'm a gentleman so I'm going to allow you a chance to clean yourself up. We're in the Upper Peninsula, but that won't do you any good because this house is miles away from anything remotely close to civilization. I have breakfast ready for you out in the kitchen. You hungry?"

"Please let me go," were my first words when the tape came off. "I want to go home."

"This is your home now." He gently helped me up from the floor. "This is your home for the rest of your life."

"What is it that you want from me?" I asked, tears forming at the corners of my eyes.

"You belong to us"—was all he said, staring out of the window.

"What the fuck does that mean?"

He said nothing.

I started crying again even harder.

Outside the room the daylight was intense. With my right hand, I shaded my eyes from the glare. He guided me through the house. It was a two-bedroom rancher with plenty of space and was decorated the way I imagined a hunter would fix up his place. To me, it was creepy. Animal heads had been stuffed and mounted on walls in the living room. A huge moose head hung over the fireplace and a bearskin rug lay on the floor in front of it. The furniture was pretty plain. The den was dark and gloomy, an almost perfect haunt for a ghoul. Denairo was that ghoul. I could still see his victim's head disappearing behind a curtain of his own blood.

Everything in the kitchen was either wood or wrought iron, pretty simple and basic. The breakfast he'd made was sitting on the table and, if the circumstances had been better, I probably would've pigged out; it looked so good. But I had already trusted him one time and had ended up God only knew where.

He escorted me to the front door and out to the huge porch.

"It's beautiful, isn't it?" he said, gesturing at the trees, shrubs, and more trees as far as the eye could see. "This is God's country."

"What do you know about God?" I asked, examining the tree line for any signs of life.

"God? Absolutely nothing. But I've sent a lot of folks to go see Him." He must've seen what I was trying to do. "Forget about it. There's nothing out there but snakes, bears, and wolves, but before you get through them, I'll pick you off—"

I was off the porch and running full speed. That's when it dawned on me, for the first time, that I wasn't wearing any shoes. Looking down at my bare feet, I lost my focus and ran between two trees and right into a briar patch full of thorns.

"Watch out for the briars!" Denairo yelled. He hadn't even stepped one foot off the porch. He stood there, laughing.

In extreme pain, I slowed down until I could find an area that was free of the stickers from hell. When I did, I collapsed to the ground in so much pain that menstrual cramps couldn't compare. I couldn't bear to look at my feet. Thorns the size of porcupine quills were nestled deeply in my skin. I howled, the pain so intense that I blacked out again.

I awakened, thinking that it was the middle of the night and I was in my own bed at my aunt and uncle's. Then, I made ready to get up and go to the bathroom and realized that I couldn't move a muscle. But I had to pee, urgently. Suddenly I remembered where I was. I was in that dark dungeon of punishment again for trying to escape to freedom. It was dark and I couldn't even see my way through to a clear thought.

I had to go bad. He hadn't taped my mouth this time.

"Please, can I go to the bathroom, please?" I begged as loud as I could, trying not to exert any more pressure on my full bladder. It felt like I was an abdominal strain away from pissing myself when the door opened. But this time the rabid glare of daylight didn't accompany Denairo. This fool came in holding a flashlight big enough to light up the entire room.

"What did I tell you would happen if you tried to run again?" he said in a chastising manner. He held the light in one hand and the knife in the other. This time I wanted him to kill me, practically begged him with my eyes.

"You didn't kill my family or friends, did you? I'm sorry, but I can't stay here for the rest of my life."

"No, you were punished enough today." He cut the ropes and stood me up.

I screamed like there was no tomorrow. Memories of the day's events came rushing back to me in waves when I stood on my badly mutilated feet. I crumpled back down to the floor in a painful heap.

"Next time you will listen to me, won't you?" He scooped me up in his arms and took me to the bathroom. He was able to carry me and angle the bright beam of light as we navigated our way through inky darkness.

The pot sitting in the middle of the bathroom floor threw me. I questioned with my eyes. I was in so much pain. Denairo gently laid me down by the pot, shining the light down at my feet. To my surprise they were wrapped up and I had been dressed in a nightgown that hung respectably down to my knees.

"I had a friend of a friend come to give you medical treatment. You'd blacked out for a while. Your feet looked worse than they really were. He seems to think you'll be as good as new in a few days. He gave you some pain medication, but that's left up to your discretion."

I glanced at the pot.

"Oh, that? That's your—how should I say—toilet facilities." He smiled, leaving the flashlight behind.

"The regular toilet doesn't work?" I asked, scared to death of the answer.

"No, Isis. Out here we live like the Amish. No hot or cold running water. No electricity. None of the comforts to which you've grown accustomed. We boil our water to take baths around here. Among other things."

I had to think about that one for a second. He'd fixed breakfast in the kitchen but, funny thing was, I never did see an actual sink.

"We're forbidden to have any contact with the outside world. Everything we need is supplied by Max. You'll meet him soon. You need clothes, Max will have a tailor come here. We're not— well, you're not to read any form of newspaper. Media is strictly taboo. Max is our only link to the outside world."

He closed the door on me, leaving me humiliated and horrified.

I didn't have a choice in the matter. It was either piss myself or use the pot. So I stood up with the thought of squatting, but my feet were too tender to put that kind of pressure on them. I had to swallow my pride and abandon proper sanitation guidelines, hike up the nightgown, and pull down the big granny panties I'd been dressed in to uncomfortably allow my butt to touch the rim of the pot. I cringed upon flesh meeting metal.

Denairo's voice came from the other side of the door. "I dressed you and—"

"I'm not trying to be rude but can you be silent until I *go*, please?" I asked, experiencing the most degrading seconds of my entire life.

"Not a problem."

I was trying to use my muscles to slow the flow of my water. I felt violated with him standing guard outside the door, possibly listening to me tinkle. It was the first week of July and already hot, but I was experiencing chills. I didn't think I was sick or anything. I wanted to die. It was my only option. Trying to escape could put someone in my family at risk. And before I'd put other people's lives in harm's way, I would take my own. I needed to find a way to make it happen. Life was funny. I'd struggled my entire senior year, trying to decide what my major would be in college. Now the ultimate decision lay in my lap. I never thought I'd be making it. I thought God would be the one to decide how I went out.

I was done and, by habit, I went to flush the toilet, almost falling off the pot. I wiped myself, feeling like the nastiest vermin that had ever reared its foul head. There was no sink water for me to wash my hands. I guessed if I couldn't come up with an adequate method of suicide, I would be dead in a month from some rogue bacteria. He had the wrong girl if he thought he could condition me for this type of living.

"I'm done," I said.

He came in and scooped me in his arms.

"Do I have to go back in there? I promise, I'll behave. I can't be alone in there."

He put me down on the mattress in the room I now referred to as the dungeon. "Are you in any pain?"

"Yes, a great deal."

"I'll bring some meds in with water."

Denairo went out and came back with bottled water and two tablets.

These are OxyContin, forty milligrams apiece," he said, handing me the pills and water. "I'll see you tomorrow. Try and get some sleep."

He walked out with the only light in the house, closing the door and surrounding me in total darkness. And in the time it would take for someone to decide what to have for dinner, the thought came to me. OxyContin would be the way out of my misery. Somewhere I remembered reading that you didn't need many. Two pills weren't enough to get the job done, but a dozen or so in one gulp would achieve the desired goal. He wasn't going to trust me with the bottle. He likely figured rationing them would keep me from doing something stupid.

I started in on Denairo three hours after he gave me the first two, whining about pain. I was hurting but not in the way my acting job suggested. He came in with two more. I faked swallowing them. He left and, three hours later, I was back at it again. Whining, crying, and complaining. The last time he came, he brought with him the coming light of a brand-new day. Sunrays swept through the dungeon. He came in carrying a breakfast tray and two pills that sat on a napkin next to a plate of eggs, bacon, and toast smeared with jam or jelly. It didn't matter to me because I wasn't eating anything.

"Thought you could use some nutrients. I hope you're good and hungry."

I shook my head. This had to be what prisoners on death row felt like during those last hours. But I didn't have hours. I was going to ingest all six pills and hope they did their magic when he left. My plan was taking too long so six would have to do the trick.

"Eat up and when you're done, I'll come back in and get you washed up."

He closed the door on my farewell tears. I prayed for God's forgiveness for taking my own life. But if I had to sacrifice myself so that this lunatic wouldn't touch my family or friends, then it was going down. I had to laugh at my little attempt at being hip. My girls would be proud. I cried for them. They would never see me again. My aunt and uncle wouldn't get closure because Denairo would dump my lifeless corpse.

The moment came and I seized it before my will faded. I swallowed the pills and lay back, waiting to taste death. I never thought of it before but I'd rather kiss its sweet lips than remain in the company of a man that made a living by it. Slowly, I drifted into the calm waves pushing me toward eternity.

I could hear voices in the distance. They didn't exactly sound like angels singing and praising the King. Sounded more like somebody arguing in a foreign language. I tried to focus but couldn't. The shapes were distorted. Fuzzy. But the light kept getting brighter as if I was heading into that bright tunnel that everybody claims to see when they're having an out-of-body experience.

"It was quite close—this one was. Good thing…this one entirely lucky," I could hear the voice of a man, dripping with a heavy accent. "Need to monitor this one," the voice sounded again.

Suddenly, my vision cleared. I was smiling and feeling like somebody had run over my head, driving an elephant. I thought

I was in Heaven and was about to see my folks, when Denairo's face detoured the plans.

"I'm beginning to think that you don't like me that much. You're pretty smart, too. I have to admit, I didn't see that one coming. Don't too much get by me. That's why I have to keep you around. But this is your last warning. The next time…I kill one of your people."

"Wh-why…why do you h-h-ave to keep me around?" I asked woozily, almost releasing tears.

Denairo smiled and said, "You belong to us."

I didn't bother to repeat myself. I figured this maniac wasn't going to give me anything else but the same line of insanity.

Later, after the elderly gray-haired doctor with the accent left, I could hear another car pull up. In walked the scariest-looking little Italian man you'd ever want to see. His eyes were creepy and I got chills from staring at him. He walked up to me and stared down like he was visually taking my measurements so I could be fitted for the last dress I would ever wear.

"Max," Denairo said, "this is *Just Isis* with no last name."

Max said nothing, just kept staring at me as if he was trying to bore a hole straight through me. His eyes were set deeply into his head and his face was marred by dents, craters, and moles. But his coldest features were those eyes. I looked away. It was like he was trying to freeze my soul or hypnotize me to keep me from trying to run.

I t was the middle of October; three months had passed since my flawed attempt at suicide.

Now I was sitting in a van parked on a hill, looking down at a club. Denairo had this crazy notion that I should attend another one of his contracted hits. I'd put up a fight, but lost when he threatened to wipe out my aunt and uncle, my friends, and their entire families. And there was absolutely no way he was letting me go. He would always answer the question behind my imprisonment; the bastard would respond with the same robotic line: "You belong to us." *Us?* What in the hell did *us* mean?

It was the dead of night. We were both dressed in black from head to toe.

We sat in a seemingly plain black cargo van in a flat, shrubby area with a clear view of Bottoms Up, a posh strip club patronized by the wealthy and powerful. Skin was the uniform for the dancers; high-end business suits for the patrons.

Denairo's special van had slots installed in one of the back doors. These slots were built to accommodate the barrel and scope of a rifle. We had about two hours until the subject would come out.

Denairo surprised me when he told me that I was going to take the shot.

"I can't shoot. I'm not a killer like you. I love life and people. You can't change me. I'm not a killer."

He laughed. "It's as easy as killing your family. Maybe I should roll on back to Detroit, and with you watching, kill the two old people one at a time, hunh?"

Tears slid down my cheeks. Desperation stained my face.

"No," I said.

"Well, that's too bad, I tell you. Okay, I have a job to do. Some of us have to work for a living. Why don't you sit up front, be a good girl, and let me earn my pay."

I did what I was told. This man was a natural-born maniac and I had to get away. He'd threatened my family numerous times before but had never followed through. I was beginning to wonder if he was simply using that as a way to control me, with no plans to actually carry out his threats. This was the perfect time to try to escape. I didn't quite know our location but the bluff where we were parked overlooked a small town. At this stage in the game, my life meant nothing to me without freedom. I would've rather died in an unfamiliar town than remain a victim in my current hell.

"I have you in my sights, Mr. Richard Dent," Denairo said from the back of the van. "The next time you might want to pay the people you borrow from."

I couldn't believe how easy it was for this man to snuff out a life. I sat in the front seat, waiting for the perfect opportunity. I glanced over my shoulder. Denairo was intently staring through the riflescope.

"Stick your head out and all your problems will soon be over," Denairo said, laughing.

And that was my cue. I opened the door and ran like my feet were on fire and the wind I generated was the only thing that could put them out. I ran through the thick brush like a jackrabbit, expecting to be gunned down any second. I heard nothing, but felt a powerful force plow into me like a runaway freight train. I fell against the trunk of a tree, struggling to catch my breath. I thought that Denairo had shot me until I saw him standing over me with a thick tree limb. That's when I realized he'd hit me with it in the left side so hard that I thought I was going to spit up a rib.

"You're starting to try my patience, Isis," he said, framed by the moonlight. It was chilly out and I could see the cold smoke bouncing off of his every word. I clutched my side in excruciating pain. Felt like my rib had torn through my chest and was threatening to rip through the light fall jacket I was wearing.

"Kill me," I begged, lying on the ground staring up at the pretty, clear, moon-filled sky, wishing that I was a part of it.

"No...I won't kill you. That would be too easy. I warned you."

He threw the tree limb into some tall grass. "Lucky for you the man known as Richard Dent is making peace with his Maker. We have to go before the local authorities arrive with dogs, helicopters, and all the resources for tracking down dangerous men like me." He scooped me into his arms and we left.

No sooner had we gotten back to the place Denairo so proudly called the Ranch in the Woods, when Max and the doctor were back. While the doctor examined me, Denairo disappeared. Max looked at me with frustration and anger in his cold eyes. He said nothing. His maintained silence scared me even more. I didn't know how he fit into this equation or why the hell I'd been brought there. So I decided to ask him. What was the worst he could to me? At that point, death would've been an improvement. I'd already tried to take my own life. I was growing fearless. A person with no fear of death is considered dangerous.

"Why am I here?" I asked Max.

I got no answer. He simply stared at me like I had lost my mind. The man took out a cigar and lit it, blowing smoke in my face like that was my answer. I wanted to hop on his back and scratch out his eyes, but something was telling me that this man wasn't a man at all. He was beyond compassion and love. Something had taken away his soul a long time ago.

"Hold, please," the doctor said in his heavy accent as I squirmed around in severe pain. "This one broke a rib."

"I had some help with this broken rib," I said, tears in my eyes. I'd never hated anybody in my life but I would make an exception for Denairo's black-hearted butt.

Max stared at me again, puffing on his annoying cigar, then shook his head and walked away.

"Why am I here?" I shouted, louder this time, growing angrier.

"Your destiny will be revealed to you later. Try to hold still until he's finished," Denairo said, stepping back into the room. The smile was gone and insanity lived in its place. I recognized the look. It was the one that I'd encountered when he'd terminated the elderly man while I watched helplessly from the rooftop.

"I warned you about your insubordination, didn't I?" he asked like I was his child. "I gave you fair warning what would happen if you kept up with your rebellious ways. Now, you've brought a world of pain to your doorstep."

My blood ran cold. It wasn't from his words, but the chilling way in which he spoke them, coupled with the look of determined death in his eyes.

"*Dottore,*" Denairo spoke in Italian, "*is lei perfetto?*"

My Italian was a little rusty. I'd taken the course as a sophomore in high school. But I think he was asking the doctor if I was ready. I just kept quiet. This was not one of those times to get lippy. Max folded his arms, puffing and staring. His face was unreadable. Denairo stood in the background, wearing an identical look.

I squirmed again as the doctor was taping my ribs. It felt like Denairo had broken my whole left side with that branch. The nasty, dark bruise left behind was proof positive.

"*Perfetto,*" the little, old, wrinkly man informed Denairo, placing the last of the tape on my wrecked ribs.

Denairo snatched me up by the arm. I cringed in pain as he pushed me toward the front door. No further words were spoken. The only noise was from the nighttime animals playing out a symphony of musical appreciation for their natural habitat.

There was a black late-model Lincoln Town Car out front. I didn't like the car the moment I laid eyes on it. There was something about this car that spoke of death. I swallowed hard as Denairo pushed me to the trunk with Max and the little doctor in tow. I had no fear for my life but I was afraid of what he was about to show me.

Denairo nodded at Max, who immediately produced the key and opened the trunk. I closed my eyes. I could see the light from the trunk through my closed eyelids. Denairo's laughter was grim and chilling. It had gotten so that I could discern his intentions through his laughter. I was visibly shaking.

"Open your eyes and stare at your punishment," Denairo ordered.

Against my will I opened my eyes to gaze upon my punishment. The burst of tears was spontaneous. The animals grew quiet as I dropped to my knees on the ground, screaming and shrieking in horror. I'd caused this to happen. My selfish need to escape was going to bring extreme grief to Tisha's family. I climbed into the trunk and hugged my friend as she lay there lifeless, eyes still open, frozen in death, seemingly staring at me in pain and blame. I screamed and hollered for my friend. She didn't deserve this. I was the guilty one. My selfishness had caused my girl her life.

"*Morte*," Max proclaimed in Italian. *Death*.

"Now you know that I keep my promises. Don't try and escape or harm yourself again. The next time I go after your other friend and her new boyfriend. *Morte*."

They dragged me away, kicking and screaming. I'd gotten my girl killed. The promise of more deaths would buy my cooperation. I had to think this thing through.

I sat in the dark recesses of my room, grieving deeply for my friend, feeling something turning inside my soul. Something was happening to me. I could feel it. The same darkness that had erased Denairo's sense of humanity was now knocking on my door. I tried to ignore it, but it kept tugging at me, showing me mental snapshots of my girl lying in the trunk with that look on her face. It forced me to remember the old man Brody had shot to death while I watched from the rooftop. The darkness that swelled in me fueled me to hate. And I hated Denairo. I would have to play his game though, and try to convince him of my transformation from docile to killer. And when I could get him to that point, I was going to kill him. Simply stated: I had to become him in order to kill him.

"*Morte,*" I said in Italian. I'd understood Max when he said it. Denairo was finished.


My first year with Denairo was like boot camp. We would rise early to work out. Judging from his training, I could see why Denairo's body looked like something off of the covers of the muscle magazines. He was sculpted, chiseled to perfection. There wasn't an ounce of body fat on his lean physique.

We would wake at the crack of dawn, despite the weather, and put in roadwork. Because we didn't have a paved road, Denairo's program involved running through the woods, through the dense thickets that would welt me up every time my bare skin brushed against them. It took some getting used to. After I saw that crying, complaining, and vomiting wasn't gonna change his mind about whipping me into shape, I stopped resisting and went ahead with his program.

Before I knew it, I'd lost pounds and gained muscle. Denairo also taught me how to correctly handle, break down, and fire a weapon. The man was like a professor with a Ph.D. in murderology. He showed me all the vital parts of the body, and showed me a lot of slides of the bodies of gunshot victims.

He would wait until it was pitch black out and show me how to maneuver without being seen. I learned martial arts and how to disable someone who had a weapon. Also, he showed me how to kill a man with one punch. I became proficient at knife-throwing. After a while, I was able to plug an apple sitting on a rock at twenty paces, dead center.

A year later, I was twenty and my body had been honed into a lethal instrument, with crisp, sharp reflexes that could react in microseconds. I still hadn't performed a contract killing. I didn't have it in me, no matter how many times I'd witnessed Denairo carry one out. I was focused on killing Denairo and him only. I wasn't going to kill for him. I was going to kill for Tisha.

The night was snowy and windy. We ate roast chicken and drank red wine. The fire crackled and popped, devouring the wooden log inside the quaint fireplace. The mood was set.

He'd trained me to be an assassin, to take life at a moment's notice. But that type of madness needed special invitation. I'd been invited when he'd kidnapped me and killed my girl. Up 'til then, I'd been prey. It was time for me to switch gears. I went into predator-mode.

So I walked over to Denairo as he ate his dinner in front of the fireplace, seductively running a finger down the side of his face. I was dressed in black sweats and a top.

"What's this?" he asked in his deep voice, pushing me away. I slipped behind him on my knees, caressing the back of his head, slipping my tongue in his ear.

He stopped eating.

"You need to walk back over to the table and finish your supper. I'm afraid I can't give you what you desire. It's not time for that. You still have a long way to go."

"Baby," I purred, "you can't take a girl away from her life and not fulfill some of her needs. I have them and I'm tired of taking care of myself."

He dropped his plate, turning around to face me. I wrapped my thick lips around my finger and began mimicking oral sex.

"I know you want me," I said, blowing in his ear. I stroked his strong jaw line with the fingers of my left hand, but I kept my right hand concealed. I kept the fork I held out of sight.

I rubbed his head, feeling him relaxing.

"You're so beautiful," he proclaimed. "I can fall in love with you in time." He closed his eyes as I passionately sucked his neck while listening to his breath becoming labored. "Yes, I can fall in love with you. Just let yourself go; eventually you'll accept your new life. We have plans for you."

I didn't stop to inquire about the plans that "we" had for me. I kept up my charade. I raised the fork in the air and tried to plunge it into the side of his neck, but Denairo's instincts were something from a Steven Seagal movie. He countered by moving with tremendous speed and catching my hand by the wrist, twisting until he possessed the fork.

"Darling, I forgive you," he said, standing me to my feet by increasing the pressure on my wrist. "I thought we talked about this kind of behavior. But now I see that you've been paying attention in class. I guess you are ready, after all. Now I'm going to have to show you who the alpha male is in this household."

"You muthafucka," I cussed, surprising myself when I said it. Profanity had come factory-issued with the brand-new black heart in my chest, created by Denairo. "I'm going to kill you like you did my girl."

"Yes. You're changing! Can you feel it? Just let it flow. The darkness is in you. But I don't like when a beautiful young lady uses bad language. I'm going to have to teach you a lesson."

Denairo put all his weight forward, forcefully bending my arm as I followed until he ended up flipping me headfirst. He dropped the fork, standing over me and undoing his pants.

I jumped to my feet and tried to kick him in the balls, but he blocked it, catching my foot and slamming me to the floor so hard that it took my breath away. I lay there, groggy and in pain. Denairo removed his pants and I wanted to run for Florida. His stiff manhood hung like he had horse in his blood.

He used long strokes with his hand, as if preparing it for action. I saw where this was going but I was too dazed to stop it. I wondered if I had a concussion, the way my head had slammed against the floor. I couldn't move. Denairo came at me and ripped my clothes off until I was naked. I tried to fight but I was too weak. My efforts failed and when he entered me, the pain was so horrible. My plan had backfired. This nigga was now trying to tear me up with his inhuman-sized dick. I wasn't gonna scream or holla, wouldn't give this bastard the satisfaction. Yeah, the shit hurt like hell, but I was a trained killer. I'd been taught to ignore pain, a feat that I was now demonstrating. While he took me, I went to that place where pain, degradation and torture couldn't follow. One thing was for sure: he would have his day in front of my gun—I was sure!

Mister Contract Killer must've had a heart. After he contacted Max, Max brought the doctor to see me. The examination was thorough as I lay on the couch feeling violated. I had a few small tears and scars, but the doctor assured me that there weren't any serious internal damages; nothing that would prevent me from having a baby.

"Baby?" I calmly said. "Have a baby by you? If I get my chance…

I'm going to kill you. You better kill me now. I'm gonna kill you."

Denairo simply laughed off the threat.

Right after the doctor finished up, I could see Max's angry eyes peering at Denairo. Max was pursing his lips and flaring his nostrils. The doctor gave me my instructions, grabbed his black doctor's bag, and walked out the front door with Max and Denairo on his heels.

It was bitterly cold outside. At the opening of the door, a chilly gust of wind blew in, disturbing the flames inside the fireplace. They closed the door and went around back, Max speaking in Italian and his voice becoming increasingly louder as they moved toward the back. I followed their voices, trying to hear what Max was saying.

I was wobbly, still in pain, but I had to listen. I stumbled to the back door and peered out the window. Max appeared to be severely reprimanding Denairo about something. I could hear bits and pieces. Max was the shorter man but his finger was in Denairo's face. The cold wind left Max's face an apple-red. Every once in a while, Max would point to the house. I thought his little midget butt would sink in the knee-deep snow.

I gently twisted the knob, cracking the door open slightly.

"Don't be stupid." I could hear Max speaking English for the first time in a nasal voice, cold smoke blowing off of every word. Max surprised me. His English was just that good.

"We don't do things like that. That's not our way. That's weak. And the Ganteeny family doesn't treat women that way. We kill, but we are *not* rapists." He paused to watch a jackrabbit hop through the trees. "What would your mother think? Keep your head. If you ask me, it was a terrible mistake to bring her here. But that was not my call."

Denairo stood there like a frozen statue. He hadn't said anything. He could've killed Max if he wanted, could've snapped his neck easily. He had to have strong respect for the man. I'd witnessed Denairo's lack of respect for human life firsthand.

"You have an important job coming up. So try to stay focused. We don't need any unwanted attention. And for your actions, I'm going to silence you until I'm satisfied you've regained your respect for the family name. You are not to speak, *period*. To anyone. This is the family's wish. Honor them." He patted Denairo on the shoulder as I quietly closed the door and slipped back under the covers on the sofa.

Denairo came in right after Max left. He looked a little pissed. His face was twisted like he couldn't stand being chastised.

He looked at me.

"*Mi displace,*" Denairo said in Italian.

I guess Max ordered Denairo to apologize to me.

"I humbly beg of your forgiveness," he told me. "My actions were inappropriate and this act of savagery won't be repeated. I've been silenced by the family so I'm no longer allowed to speak using my voice."

Max had ordered Denairo to apologize to me, which I knew didn't sit too well with Denairo. But as far as Max silencing him, I didn't care if he ever spoke to me again. You didn't need to dialogue with somebody when you killed them. Denairo's days were numbered.

Later on that year, I found myself in Chicago driving a limousine. Denairo was still under family-ordered silence and hating it. I'd gotten good at reading him, and whatever I couldn't figure out, he wrote down. I still wasn't good enough to match his combat skills, but I was growing more confident with every self-defense move that I mastered.

I was a chauffeur, complete with black hat, suit, and gloves. My client was a tall, chubby-faced man named Clifford Watcher. Clifford ran a successful large company called Watcher Enterprise. He was the biggest businessman in Chicago, with a string of Businessman-of-the-Year awards. A great man who came from humble beginnings, Clifford was the youngest of ten kids. He had grown up poor on the city's South Side. But he had soon overshadowed his siblings, excelling academically and athletically.

His academic and athletic prowess had soon caught the eyes of recruiters from the University of Michigan. He'd been there for two years before being approached by an Italian man in a flashy business suit. Like the old saying goes, he was made an offer he couldn't refuse.

He was approached and given money to start a company building gizmos and trinkets. Inside of two years, he'd managed to build the company into a multimillion-dollar industry. Business was so good that the company expanded, opening headquarters in other states. Then Watcher had a brainstorm—horseracing. With some help from the powers that be, he built a racetrack in Chicago. But he eventually found out that his silent partners were using his company for illegal activities: money laundering; drugs; gambling.

Enraged, Clifford threatened to expose all. And that's why Denairo and I were in the city of Chicago, picking up Clifford from a posh hotel on Michigan Avenue.

My assistance was mandatory. I wasn't given a choice. I didn't want to risk being marched outside again and seeing another one of my loved ones lying dead in a trunk. My cooperation was vital to ensure their survival. It seemed like Tisha's death had a profound impact on my emotions. My grief for her had opened my eyes to the barbarity of this cold and cruel world. In short, I had no more tears to cry. Tears were for the weak. And I couldn't afford to be weak while keeping company with a wolf.

This was to be a two-man operation with me replacing Clifford Watcher's usual driver. I felt sorry for the elderly black chauffeur. Denairo had put two in the man's head in an alley shortly after carjacking him. So there I was, sitting behind the wheel of a limousine. Denairo was six cars behind me on the same side, behind the wheel of an expensive-looking tow truck.

My heart was thumping wildly. Clifford Watcher was taking so long that I almost pulled off a couple of times. But Tisha's cold death-stare was enough to make me stay put.

It was summer and people were everywhere—coming and going, shopping and sightseeing. This was the only time I got to see people going about their everyday lives. Why couldn't I have a normal life? I wanted to open the door and talk to somebody. But I had no right to put somebody's life in danger. I didn't want Denairo to assume that I was trying to be cute and asking for help on the sly. And no matter if I tried to convince him that there'd been only small talk, Denairo would track down that person and terminate them. So I kept quiet.

I could see Denairo through the driver's side mirror. I waited for a few more moments. Then I saw Clifford come out, chatting with the doorman. I swallowed my fear and got out of the car. I could see Denairo smirking, laughing. Killing someone always brought out his amused side.

"My, my, my," Clifford said, staring tastefully at me as I opened the door, "you are a pretty young woman."

"Thank you," I said, blushing slightly. I closed the door and slid behind the wheel. In spite of his chubby face and body, Clifford had a dazzling smile, a perfect set of pretty white teeth, and he seemed friendly enough.

"What's the matter, gorgeous?" Clifford said. "Super-modeling jobs hard to come by?" He laughed.

I had to give it to the man. He had no game, but his bank

account more than made up for what he lacked in conversation skills.

I smiled. "Thank you for the compliment."

Through the rearview mirror, I could see him trying to think of something catchy to say. It was hard to believe this man was the CEO of a company like Watcher Enterprise. He was actually struggling with holding a conversation. I didn't mind. Compared to the hell I was living in, this guy was coming off like Don Juan.

I hit a couple of corners and we were headed toward the racetrack. I was really enjoying our conversation until the tow truck appeared in my rearview mirror. Reality hit me. On cue, I went into my showbiz routine, pulling over to the shoulder of the two-lane highway we were traveling.

"What's wrong, honey?" he asked, still smiling.

"A little car trouble." I opened the door. "Please stay in the car, Mr. Watcher. The situation is under control." I offered him my best smile. Clifford Watcher blew me a kiss. I made like I caught it. "Thank you."

I raised the hood, signaling that I was in distress. Minutes later, the tow truck pulled over in back. Clifford Watcher didn't deserve this. His only crime was trying to live right. But he'd pissed off a lot of people. My feelings about it told me that I wasn't turning into a cold-blooded killer. I just wanted to get in the car and drive; take Clifford Watcher far away. He didn't deserve this. None of Denairo's victims had. This man had executed some prominent black men, too. Good black men were already hard to come by and there he was killing off the crème de la crème, the cream of the crop. But Denairo was an equal opportunity hit man, with the philosophy that death amounted to wealth.

Denairo exited the truck, whistling while he walked toward the limousine.

"Who are you?" I heard Clifford Watcher ask in a startled voice when Denairo casually opened the door.

Seconds later, I heard screaming. I stood outside, trying not to imagine what was going on inside the car. The struggle going on between the two men caused the limo to rock. Clifford Watcher was screaming like a girl. But the scream was cut short, dying inside his throat. Afterward, Denairo emerged, smiling.

Blood stained his gray mechanic's uniform shirt. His hands were wrapped in barbed wire. The wire had embedded into the skin of his hands, drawing blood. I could imagine the force used to kill Clifford Watcher. Blood and chunks of meat dangled on some of the spikes. It was sickening. The bruise underneath Denairo's right eye meant Clifford Watcher hadn't gone out without a struggle. This was my first experience being this close up while Denairo carried out a termination. I had a feeling that it wouldn't be the last.

Gesturing with his head, he ordered me inside the truck. I obeyed. Denairo hooked the limo up, then slid behind the wheel of the truck. The two-lane highway was desolate as dusk settled over the area. Denairo pulled off the shoulder and we disappeared into the approaching darkness. His brilliant megawatt smile of death spoke volumes.

I felt bad for Clifford Watcher. He seemed to be a good brother. Denairo was a gargoyle and needed to be put down. For years he'd operated in the shadows, killing from a distance. Most of his victims had never seen it coming. Local and state authorities were oblivious to his brand of underworld civilized terror. He didn't exist. He was almost like a vampire lurking in the twenty-first century. But instead of for blood, he slaughtered for the thrill. It wasn't really about money. He had a blood lust that only death could quench.

It's been said that environment influences human behavior and nurtures development. You are the reflection of your friends and associates. For years now, I'd been living with a contract killer and I was rapidly losing my identity, becoming another *something* that the world could do without. And if it was the last thing in this world that I did, I was going to kill that black-hearted bastard...or die trying.

It was a lovely spring day. It was April, but I had lost track of the date. I had been gone from civilization for four years now. Though I tried to bury the memories of my past, sometimes they wouldn't stay that way. I often thought about Auntie Ruthie Jean and Uncle Jim, wondering if they were still alive. Something in my heart told me that they were no longer physically of this world, leaving me with tremendous heartache.

The days were long but the nights were even longer. This Amish way of living was deplorable. I was tired of relieving myself over a pot and taking baths inside an old rusty tin tub. I wanted to live life like a woman again—hang with my girls at the mall, go get manicures and pedicures. I wanted to be desired at the bar by drooling men standing in line to see which one I would let buy me a drink. I wanted to live my life without being frightened into assisting with death and destruction.

The simple desire to go to a restaurant and sit at a table with a menu and fine cuisine that hadn't been freshly hunted down and killed, pushed me into wandering through the woods one day in search of civilization. I wished that I could truly express what made me walk off. I simply wanted to live like a normal girl again and be pampered.

A half hour later, I was confused and disoriented, staring in every direction at trees and woods that all looked the same. I was lost. Denairo had gone to the cellar when I'd started walking. Aimlessly I'd strolled off, growing more confused with each step. The birds were chirping and singing sweet songs of freedom to me. I thought the squirrels running about playing Tag through the leaf litter were so cute. I wanted to play. So I gave chase but they were so fast that I was soon out of breath, dropping to the ground to have a conversation with the earthworms. I listened to them report that the little green people from Mars were due to come back with Christopher Columbus and rediscover America.

I must've laughed a ton with my new friends. I didn't even care that I'd left wearing only a dark-colored housecoat and white tennis shoes. The only other thing I could hear was a constant rattle. I couldn't quite make it out. It reminded me of a baby rattle. I was no longer scared. The animals were my friends. So I started throwing leaves up in the air, some of them landing in my hair with the dirt. I ran my hands in my hair to give it that frizzy look. I was trying to emulate the fuzzy animal that had scurried off underneath the brush.

"Come here, my friend," I said, giving chase.

The baby rattle was getting so loud it drowned out all other sounds. Over to the left, by a big tree, I could see a snake. He was making the baby-rattle noise. I simply strolled up to Mister Snake to tell him that he need not fear and, when I reached to milk him, he bit my hand.

The pain didn't start until I walked away. But immediately after, I was crying and wanting my momma. I was growing tired and sat next to a tree, thinking, *Wouldn't it be great to be a raccoon?* before I drifted off to sleep.

I woke the next day. The little Italian doctor was back. Max and Denairo were standing over the couch. Denairo was without movement or emotion, as usual. Max had a disgusted look on his lemon-shaped face.

"You stupid, undisciplined bitch," he hissed. It sounded like his nasal passages were swollen to twice their normal size. "You could've attracted some serious attention to yourself. Could've cost us big." His face was a couple inches from mine. "I should've let your stupid ass die."

Denairo just stood there, looking stone-faced.

"This one get plenty rest," the doctor explained in a gruff Italian accent, handing Max a pill bottle. "This was lucky. Could been dead." He grabbed his black bag and hat. "She should take twice a day. She has nervous breakdown. Too much stress. Need lots of rest, this one does."

"All I wanted was a cheeseburger," I babbled, not even knowing that my mouth was moving. "Can somebody tell me why I'm here with the Three Stooges?"

Max calmed down a little after the doctor explained that I'd suffered a nervous breakdown. Being exposed to that much death wasn't natural for anyone. Max said something to Denairo in Italian. They followed the doctor out the door. I was left to ponder. My hand was sore, but the doctor informed us that the snake had given me a dry bite, meaning it hadn't injected venom. Denairo came back in and gave me some pills with water. I wish that I could say what happened next, but I dozed off.

I was on the shelf for four months. Shortly after, I was fully activated and our latest caper would be one for the record books. We had gotten our orders directly from Max. The old man wouldn't tell me much, only the objective. Denairo was supposed to take out some big-time, loud-mouthed gangsta rapper by the name of 187—police code for murder. The arrogant superstar had recorded a few songs to maim mafia brass: "Mafia, These Nuts" and "Snuff by Nigga Necktie."

His lyrics were harsh and to the point, and he would proclaim to be the greatest rapper of all time. 187 didn't have to do too much bragging; his many platinum hits backed him up. But still he boasted about how he was so much better than the late Tupac Shakur or The Notorious B.I.G.

The foot in the mouth came when he claimed to have murdered the head of a mafia family. That was a major slap in the face to the powers that be. They'd had enough of the Long Beach gangbanger-turned-rapper. He'd overstepped his boundaries. Denairo was called in. 187's recording contract had been signed in ink, but the contract on his life would be signed with his blood. I didn't condone killing but I couldn't say he didn't bring it on himself.

Another Black man was about to feel Denairo's wrath. And as usual, I was powerless to stop the hit. I was sorry, but I'd gotten to the cold-hearted point of rationalizing it as better them than one of my loved ones. I went along without friction.

187 would kick off his latest concert tour at Detroit's Ford Field. He was promoting his new album, *187 on a Mafia Nigga*. They got me a job working security. My mission was to screen the spectators for weapons. I was such a hypocrite. Here I was screening, ensuring the safety of the entertainers and patrons, but turning a blind eye to Denairo's merciless blood-and-guts agenda. My handheld metal detector had been rigged so the wand wouldn't register anything. Not only was I letting Denairo through with a high-powered rifle, but probably a whole lot of other folks carrying weapons as well. I didn't like it. The termination had to go down, but if any audience members got injured by another gun-toting patron, I probably would've hung myself.

As the crowds thickened, I wanted in the worst way to go to somebody and ask for help. But I couldn't; I was being watched.

Among the swarm of happy hip-hoppers lurked surveillance

for the mob. These were real nasty individuals who would kill for the sport. So I did the job. I perked up as a crowd of energized teenagers came through my line, trying to pick me up. Their little hormones were way out in outer space. Denairo had no problem blending in. His boyish looks allowed him to pass as a punk in his late-teen years.

I waved my broken wand until the last hip-hopper was through. I had a minute before show time so I went to the bathroom to pray, not for myself but for 187.

Inside the arena, 187 huffed and puffed, sweating profusely. He was a massive individual with a huge round head. Dark chocolate to the bone, 187 stood about six-foot-six. His hands resembled catcher's mitts as they embraced the microphone. He energetically moved from one side of the stage to the other, waving his free hand, yelling the traditional, "Wave your hands in the air."

His voice was gruff, yet hypnotic. Everything about 187 screamed out roughneck, from his highly starched khakis to his hoodlum mannerisms. A thick, white-gold chain draped his neck. From where I was sitting—or should I say standing, 'cause no one sat at a rap concert—I couldn't make out the medallion. It swayed from side to side with his movements.

The crowd was hyped, loud, yelling for 187 to perform at that level. I gazed around the crowd of black and white faces, wondering where Denairo would be setting up for the kill shot. I scanned the rafters for any flashes of metal.

I'd been to a couple of rap concerts and had never observed the DJ mixing and scratching while wearing an execution-style hood on his head. That struck me as a bit odd. Curiously, I asked around, inquiring about the DJ. All the answers were the same. They explained to me that DJ Hood wore the black hood to honor all his gangbanger homies that he'd lost to capital punishment. It was his trademark. I had to admit that it was one creative gimmick.

The crowd pumped fists, sang along, danced, and yelled right along with 187. He'd sung almost every song on the new album. Going into his final song, 187 stopped to introduce a few new acts he'd signed to his new label, Two to da Head Records: a female rapper by the name of Time Bomb, and a group known as the Dysfunctional Two. While the new artists walked off the stage, 187 told everybody to look out for their upcoming CDs.

"Now," he said, wiping sweat away from his brow, "are you muthafuckas waitin' on this dope shit?"

The crowd went nuts, responding with screams and wolf-whistles.

"187 was savin' this shit for the end!" he screamed into the microphone. "Killin' muthafuckin' mobsters is how I'm 'bout to begin! Killin' punk-ass mobsters is how I put it down! So put your fuckin' hands in the air and check out these fresh-ass sounds!

"Here we go…here we go!" he yelled, skipping across the stage, almost creating a riot. "187 is the name, killing mob bosses is my game…"

He didn't get a chance to finish as his body was suddenly jerked clear off of his feet and violently thrown backward, almost like a car had struck him head-on. A wave of silence passed through the crowd as 187's body bounced once off of the stage floor before coming to rest.

The crowd was stunned. They didn't know if this was scripted or if the rapper had experienced some type of blackout. But I understood. Denairo's superb marksmanship had put 187 on his back.

Suddenly the crowd began to stir as they realized that 187 wasn't getting up. It took one person in the front row to recognize the small pool of blood trailing from the rapper's body and to yell, "Shit, 187's been shot!"

All hell broke loose. Screams pierced the air. People frantically pushed and shoved, trampling poor, unfortunate souls who fell to the floor.

I was running for my life. I thanked God that I wasn't caught up in the thick of the crowd. I had gotten a jump on everybody. But I wasn't swift enough to outrun some of the track stars that had caught up. I was bounced around like a ball inside a pinball machine. I had to stay on my feet. I couldn't fall. Couldn't afford to. My little body would be crushed.

As far as I was concerned, Denairo would be the one to blame for my death. He'd caused the stampede. A heavyset kid with bad acne slammed into me, spinning me around so that I was facing in the direction of the stage. I ducked a couple of more frantic people, somehow getting my stride back on track.

Once outside, I escaped into the darkness. I ran all the way to the rendezvous spot. Denairo sat in the back of a stretch Hummer limo. We drove off into the inky blackness of the night.

187 had gotten his. I was sure Denairo had left a calling card on the body, making sure the mob had gotten their point across to the rappers: leave the Italian Mafia out of the rap world of rhyming and murderous lyrics.

I was twenty-four years old now but I'd stopped celebrating birthdays a long time ago. They were for people who cherished life, celebrating one more year of God's blessings. I, on the other hand, had nothing to celebrate.

Max had long since released Denairo from his original punishment of silence, but Denairo's tendency to always want to do things his way had kept him at odds with Max. Max would always resort to suspending Denairo's speaking privileges. This was just another one of those incidences. Denairo had gotten himself in hot water for setting up a hit his way and now he was mute again.

On a warm night, nearing nightfall, we'd finished eating and were sitting around, lounging in the house when Max paid us a routine visit. Denairo had caught a couple of rabbits, skinned them, and roasted them over an open fire in the kitchen.

Max's face was kind of red. He was wearing the granddaddy of all dumbfounded looks. I was surprised to see Max there so late; he usually made his rounds in the morning. Something about it smelled wrong.

He came in and walked right past me, zombie-like. He whispered to Denairo, then they went outside. They weren't gone but a couple of minutes before they walked back inside. They both stood over me with strange looks on their faces.

"We have a hit for you. You must kill the bishop of Mount Holy Church," Max explained. "We want you and Denairo to pose as a couple looking to wed. That's how you're going to get close. Kill him right when the ceremony is being performed. We've already made arrangements for the ceremony. The bishop is the only witness in a criminal case that could send one of ours away for good. He's a made guy and part of the Santinie family."

I was stunned. Now I also looked dumbfounded. Like a deer caught in the headlights.

"The bishop is known for having his men around the church. Kill him and get out, *quickly*." He turned his back to us. "Be ready next week. We're on a very tight timetable."

With that said, he stepped out into the rural night and left in his shabby old Ford Bronco. I felt like I'd been sold on the slave blocks. Denairo went into the kitchen and had a second helping of rabbit. He showed absolutely no emotion, just sat there at the table and feasted on his rabbit like Max had never dropped by with that announcement.

One more life to take, more hearts to break, I figured.

We were chauffeured to a huge chapel. The chapel was warm, inviting. We weren't decked out in the traditional garb. It was simple everyday wear. We had been told nothing spectacular, no glitz or glamour. I was extremely nervous. A man of God would be added to Denairo's long list of cemetery markers.

I could taste the tension in the air. We were led in through a door and down the aisle directly to the altar. I didn't get the opportunity to march down the aisle while the musician belted out a beautiful rendition of "Here Comes the Bride."

I nervously glanced around from pew to pew, door to door, and from Denairo to the chubby-faced, itty-bitty white minister. My hands were moist with perspiration.

Denairo was unusually fidgety. On several occasions, I'd caught him surveying the room, possibly looking for a way to escape. Now he was looking from left to right like he was at a tennis match. I was giddy, Denairo was on edge, but the minister never stopped talking. He was dressed in traditional minister attire: a long, black, flowing robe, outlined in gold. Two medium-sized crucifixes decorated the right and left breasts of the robe.

I was caught in a fog. This ceremony couldn't be happening. The scene wasn't real. I kept trying to wake myself from this bad nightmare. At any moment, I expected to wake up snug in my bed with my aunt and uncle staring down at me, smiling.

"Isis, now," Denairo said under his breath. "Do it...now."

I'd been given a 9mm back in the car and it was tucked in the small of my back. So Denairo pulled his, shot, and missed as the minister dove for cover. That was when it hit the fan.

Doors flew open and masked men burst through, all equipped with automatic rifles. I took cover behind a gigantic pillar.

A gunfight erupted. Over my head, to the right and left of me, I could hear feet shuffling in a mad attempt to take cover.

The wall I was lying next to was riddled with bullets. Smoke was everywhere. Crumbling plaster fell to the ground and I was covered by a white chalky film. I couldn't see Denairo or the minister. The barrage of automatic gunfire let me know that Denairo was still alive. Bullets thumped the wall. Dust was thick in the air, hindering my vision.

I was afraid to stick my head out to take a quick peek. I'd seen what a bullet could do to the human head. It wasn't a pretty sight. It sounded like a war was being waged over my head.

I offered up a prayer, hoping God would deliver me. I was so deeply into meditation, I barely heard as an unfamiliar voice screamed, "Oh my God, I've been shot!" Then a couple of seconds later, the same scream was repeated, but in a different voice.

Each crackle from the automatic weapons made me wish that I were invisible, totally transparent to the naked eye. Something clicked inside me. Denairo always described it as a switch being flipped and the training kicking in. Well, that's exactly what happened. All that I had been through since my abduction was used for fuel—my aunt and uncle; Tisha's death; the nervous breakdown. I grew dizzy with anger.

Throwing caution to the wind, I slowly peeked out, a bullet whizzing by my face. I saw that the minister's men were armed with bigger weapons than I'd imagined. From first look, there seemed to be at least six of them. Denairo was pinned down behind a heavy cement column. Bullets pinged and ponged, embedding into the cement.

He was holding them at bay. I realized the 9mm pistol he was firing wouldn't hold them off for long. I had to think and think fast. Denairo was all I had. If they killed him, I would have no chance at survival. Because I'd jumped to the floor so fast, the men probably thought I'd gotten hit. So now they were focusing on Denairo, which meant I had the element of surprise on my side. There were so many of them. My mind fired on all cylinders. My pulse quickened, igniting my adrenaline. Putting myself in harm's way, without even thinking about it, I shot up from my hiding spot, screaming like I was insane. The distraction worked, drawing attention to me, and off of Denairo for the moment.

"Get that bitch," I heard one of them curse from behind his mask. Denairo shot him first. The man's face disappeared behind dark blood-splashes and powder-burned wool. One down; five to go.

As swift as I could, I dove back to my hiding spot and took out my pistol, ready for war, and just in time. Bullets splintered what used to be a wooden podium.

A quick peep revealed confusion, a disruption in the ranks. Before, they'd seemed to be well-organized and overconfident in their numbers. Now, after the death of the first one, they looked like amateurs. I assumed that the first one killed was the boss.

"A, B," one of them spoke, "ya'll get the tramp."

In all the confusion, two of the men broke away from the pack, heading toward me. I racked back the slide of my weapon, readying it, but the stupid thing jammed on me. I had to think fast. I couldn't panic. *Play dead; play dead*, I thought.

The two masked men reached me. Carefully, they peered over at me. I lay still, deathly still.

"She's dead already," one said in a heavy Italian accent.

"Check her closely," the second commanded. He dropped to his knee to get my pulse. It was as if I had no control over my body. It didn't even give me a moment's notice. My eyes opened as the palm of my right hand smashed upward into his nose. I heard a disgusting crunching sound behind the mask, felt the bones in his nose grind up into his head.

The only sound he made was when his lifeless body dropped to the floor with a thud.

"*Morte!*" I yelled out.

"You bitch," said the second one.

It didn't matter; my adrenaline was pumping so fast, I was on him before he could raise his weapon. My body reacted like a lethal weapon.

I grabbed the barrel of his automatic, pulling it to me with so much force, his body couldn't do anything but follow. A swift and smooth kung fu chop to the Adam's apple separated his spirit from his body. With stealthy precision, I picked up the dead man's weapon, held it tight, squeezing off three rounds before diving back to my hiding spot. The other goons were hard to hit. They were safely concealed by the wooden pews.

"Somebody get that bitch!" one of the remaining three screamed in frustration.

The idiot made the misfortune of standing in the open while he shouted. The next sounds I heard from him were gurgles. Denairo had shot him in the throat. He dropped like a boulder from the sky.

One of the last two yelled out, "Shit, let's get out here!" His English was horrible.

Denairo shot one last time at the retreating couple, injuring one of them in the leg.

In the wake of what should've been the perfect hit, dust, empty shell casings, dead bodies, and lots of insurance damage remained.

I dropped my weapon and cried like a baby, thinking I could've been killed. Hell, I'd killed people, something I'd sworn never to do. This was self-defense, but I still felt bad. After all, I wasn't an animal. My heart went out to the men lying dead on the floor. They were fathers, sons, husbands, uncles, nephews. But now they were dead. You don't really get a chance to think in the heat of battle, but now, nothing but gloom and shadow remained.

"Pretty impressive," a creepy voice congratulated me.

The voice didn't register at first. When I slowly looked up, I saw that the minister wasn't dead, nor had he fled. Instead, he was standing over me, clutching a nickel-plated pistol. With his chubby little red fingers, he pulled me up by my hair.

Holding me tightly by my neck, his pistol at my temple, he yelled, "Show yourself!"

The demand forced Denairo into the open. He wasn't alone though. He also gripped his pistol.

"Who sent you to kill me?" the minister shouted the question.

I said nothing, just focused on breathing. The freak had his arm wrapped so tightly around my neck, I was struggling for air. Once again, I'd been put in a compromising position. Denairo stood there in the aisle like Dirty Harry with his gun down by his leg. His eyes stared deeply into mine. I don't know how I figured him out, but I did.

"Let this be a lesson to anybody else looking to put a price on my head," the minister declared, looking around at his fallen helpers. "Tonight, you die."

He aimed the gun at Denairo, and right on cue, I tried to bite a plug out of the hand nearest my mouth. The minister let me go to grab his bleeding hand. Bad move. Denairo split his head in half with one shot.

We had no time to talk—not that I would get much out of Denairo anyway. We fled the scene before the police arrived.

Max picked us up around the corner in an older-model cargo van with no windows. On the way home, he drilled us with question after question. The bastard wanted all the gory details. Max rattled on the whole time.

I looked at Denairo. He was favoring his left wrist. He didn't tell me, but I knew he'd been grazed in the gun battle. Of course, he didn't have anything to add to the conversation. He just sat there in deep thought.

I couldn't see which route we were traveling. Emotionally, I was drained. I'd killed and now I really didn't know what to make of it. I could kill again, if I was cornered. Denairo had finally transformed me into a killer, the perfect weapon. I'd tasted my first drop of blood, and now I wondered if I would develop some insatiable appetite for it. But even with all my special skills, I was still no match for the teacher.

A couple of days after the mission, Denairo came at me again with that look in his eyes. I knew what he wanted, but he was going to have to take it over my dead body. The physical confrontation was brutal. And even though I managed to draw blood, he was able to subdue me, raping me again.

"Shit!" I screamed in agonizing pain. Denairo had managed to get me pregnant by raping me twice more after the church mission. Once I found out that I was with child and abortion wasn't an option, I turned suicidal. And once again I was watched, for nine months this time, until today.

This pig-looking, pudgy Italian white lady said, "*Push*. I see head—push."

"Push, hell, get this kid out of me," I retorted.

"Bear down now. I need you, push," she said in a heavy Italian accent. "I see head of *bebe*, push, push."

The crying was instantaneous. Kids can really come out crying from the joy of birth or the sorrow of being born into a life of sin. Max had brought in the little Italian lady. I'd asked why I couldn't have a normal hospital delivery and Max yelled at me to keep quiet.

I had mixed feelings. The baby was mine but I'd been raped and violated, and felt like my body was no longer mine. It belonged to the Ganteenys and whatever sick and twisted plans they harbored. How was I supposed to act? I had my fantasy about babies being born from the unconditional love of two consenting adults. There was no love, nor had my consent produced this kid. And as far as I was concerned, this baby carried the unstable, violent gene of a man who worshiped the deadly art of killing.

But as much as I wanted to hate my baby boy, I found myself drawn by his crying.

The little lady was cleaning my baby, taking her time, holding the child like it was her own. Something about her freaked me out. She spoke in Italian to the baby, kissing its forehead and eyeing me strangely. I realized something was wrong when she handed the crying bundle of joy over to Max instead of me. I was petrified.

"Can I hold my baby, please?" I yelled. Instead of complying, Max stared at me as if I ought to know my place. "Give me my baby, please." The two ignored me and continued their conversation in Italian.

Denairo stared quietly out of the window. I'd heard stories about the Italian culture, about the sex of the baby. How mobsters partied when their babies turned out to be male. As with many cultures, the male baby was looked upon as the one who would carry on the family name. It was especially imperative that Italian crime families had as many male children as possible. The strength of their families depended on men for survival and dominance.

I wasn't stupid. Max was the real deal and my baby had Italian blood running through its veins, and I feared the worst. Denairo had never told me his story. But looking at him, I'd put it together. He was half-Italian. I didn't know a lot about his parents but I guessed that he was taken from his mother, just as they were about to try to take my baby.

The clock sitting on the mantle let me know my baby was born at exactly 11:05 p.m. Not that any of that mattered, because no birth records would be recorded. To the world, my child wouldn't exist. Hell, Denairo didn't exist. I'd noticed one night while he was sleeping that his fingertips were smooth. Nothing resembling a fingerprint could be detected. I didn't quite know what procedure had been used, but Denairo had nothing that could be traced back to him. I wondered if his being a half-breed had anything to do with his garbage man position in the family. I feared for my baby. Feared my baby was lost.

I was cleaned up and put to bed. They still kept my baby from me. I almost cried myself to sleep. It wasn't a surprise that Max and the little Italian lady stayed the night. Later, the little Italian lady came to me, holding a cup of water. I swung at her.

"I don't want any damn water! I just want my baby, you bitch!" But I was exhausted, and eventually she got me to calm down and drink the water.

Suddenly, I grabbed my throat.

"You bitch!" I screamed. I was seeing double. I lunged at her, falling off the couch to the floor, grabbing at her foot. "Gimme my baby! I want my baby!" I yelled before whatever was in the water kicked in, sending me to sleep.

I woke up to an empty house. Everybody was gone. I swallowed hard. Everybody, including my baby. My heart ached and my spirit cried the tears of a mother who'd lost her firstborn. Even though I'd given birth to a live baby, there was no telling what deeds of death Max had in store for my child.

For a day or two, I sat on the couch with my knees pulled up to my chin, rocking back and forth like I was in a trance. I sat that way, my eyes fixated on the door like Denairo and Max were due to walk in with my baby in arms. I couldn't even form tears to cry. I'd been used and abandoned.

Around day three, I got the urge to walk around, pacing back and forth like a wild panther in a cage, thinking about how it had felt to be free before I was kidnapped. I had no desire for food, water, or anything else. My baby troubled my mind. I never thought I could feel that way for another human being. But the miracle of birth was something one had to experience to totally appreciate.

My baby was a part of me and I was a part of my baby; flesh of my flesh and blood of my blood. The urgency to find my infant was overwhelming. So in the diminishing daylight, I set about gathering my clothes and supplies. The way I had it figured, Max and Denairo had a three-day advantage.

I was fidgeting around with the fastener of a green army back-pack when I saw something that resembled a letter. It sat on a bookshelf atop some hardbacks. It had to be from Denairo. My three-day stupor had prevented me from seeing it before. It was addressed to me. The confessions were startling.

My eyes were riveted to every word, every sentence. It was so heartfelt; I could hear his voice, like he was narrating the thing:

*Isis, I don't know where to begin. But I'll start out by saying that I'm sorry for everything I put you through. It was just the stress of the job. I had to lie down with the guilt of tearing up your life every single night. Your father was a senior accountant for the Ganteeny family. An audit showed that he had been embezzling funds. A price went out on his head and the murder was staged to look like a traffic accident. And even though the bosses killed your father and mother, your father still was left with an outstanding balance. You were expected to make the final payment. That is why I kept referring to you as 'belonging to us.' The night I met you at the club, men were sent to your house to kill your uncle and aunt. Isis, I am so sorry for your friend Tisha, too, but I was just following orders. I know you have a lot of questions and I'm gonna do my best to answer them for you. My mother gave birth to me under the watch of a midwife, similar to what you went through. I was born to be made into the perfect weapon because there were no legal documents on file about my birth. That was the way it was designed. Max is my father and because I was born mixed, the only job available inside the family was that of assassin. With no history I could move around in the shadows, under the radar of law enforcement. When I became of age, Max took me from my mother and moved me to this house in the woods. It was the perfect location to train a killer. Max said that I should learn to live without all the necessities of modern life because it would make me better at my job. A few years had gone by when I found out that Max had had my mother murdered. It's all a*

*vicious cycle. They always need new blood at this position. They abduct
women, get them pregnant, and steal the babies—provided the child is
male. I don't even want to tell you about the actions they take if the
baby is a girl. All babies are born using a midwife. And like they did
my mother, they kill the women after birth, so I'm warning you to
please get out of the house. Down in the cellar, there's a door. There's
a stash of weapons in the room. Quickly, they're coming for you. I tried
to talk them out of it, but it was determined that you knew too much.
You've been trained. Kill as many as you can get and get the hell out.*

    *Love ya, Denairo.*

    *Your Al Pacino.*

I didn't have time to hate Max and the Ganteeny family. My
legs must've forgotten that my brain was in charge; I was in the
cellar so fast, I didn't quite remember walking down the stairs.
The only thing I could remember was opening the door and seeing a room that looked like something out of a James Bond
movie. The weapons ranged from large to small. Any type you
could name. The only source of light was a kerosene lantern
burning brightly, sitting atop an ancient desk. The weapons were
neatly stored in a weapons rack, hanging on three of the walls.

For a jaw-dropping moment, I stood dazed by the ominous-
looking arsenal. But light creeping in from the floorboards above
me let me know that I wasn't alone. I'd heard the sounds of the
house settling before, but these creaks were different. These
sounds were being made by sneaky feet, and judging by the number of creaks, it was safe to say that there were many. They were
tiptoeing.

I felt trapped like a rat. And almost on cue, one of my old friends
scurried from behind a massive wooden crate. Another creak
came from overhead. They knew I was down here. They would

be storming down there soon. I didn't have time to think. That's when I remembered that I'd left my supplies upstairs. I couldn't do anything about it now. So, without hesitation, I grabbed a gray duffel bag, filling it with ammunition.

Then I grabbed for weapons. I tucked two Glocks into the waistband of my sweatpants. At that time, another rat scurried from behind the crate. Curiosity led me to peep behind it. I could see a door with faint daylight streaming through the crack underneath. A way out! Suddenly, everything was looking up. It didn't look like I would have to shoot my way out. So with no time to lose, I grabbed a crowbar, inserting the sharp end between the crate and door, straining and struggling to pry the thing open. I was nearly to the point of soiling my pants when I heard the tremendous crash as the crate hit the floor. Time was of the essence. The men upstairs had heard what I did and I could hear their footsteps nearing the cellar door. That's why I didn't think twice about shooting the padlock off.

The thing gave way and fell to the floor as the door popped open. It seemed to be some kind of trapdoor leading to the outside. I guessed it was a way to transport coal into the cellar. But for now, it was my escape route. Slinging the automatic assault rifles over both shoulders and holding one at the ready, I wondered about how many men were posted outside. It was either take my chances with the goons in the house, or the trapdoor.

No doubt these goons were egotistical fools who probably underestimated the resilience of a woman. Once again, I had the element of surprise working for me. I could hear them in the weapons room. But I was moving slowly up the stairs.

Daylight was right beyond the double doors. I wasn't that big so I pushed open one door, holding it as I pushed it back as far as it could go. I carefully popped my head out, noticing nobody was outside standing guard. But what if they had snipers posted in the trees? I reasoned if they were, I would've been toast by now. I threw myself up and out of the trapdoor.

By this time, my fear had turned to stone-cold hatred. The nerve of those bastards, taking my baby and now here they were, sneaking around trying to kill me. The hatred alone caused me to stand beside the open door, concealed from my pursuers.

I held my breath, pulling one of the Glocks out. When he emerged from the trapdoor, the jerk looked like I'd imagined him. Like one of the goons at the wedding ceremony. Same black masked face. Same black suit. He didn't see me holding the Glock at his temple.

Driven solely by a will to live and to seek revenge for the baby I hadn't seen, I pulled the trigger. Blood splattered on my army green sweatshirt as I watched brain matter and blood mist spray wildly through the air. The creep looked at me with dazed eyes as he rocked back and forth, like I had no right to take his life. I didn't have time to play. I helped him by pushing his head, watching him tumble down the trapdoor stairs, ending up on the landing with a sickening *thud*. The punk landed crumpled up at the feet of one of his companions, who yelled obscenities. The next thing I heard was gunfire as one of the assassins looked up and spotted me insanely smiling down on him.

I dashed madly through the woods, not knowing where I was going. As I ran, dodging the trees, I could hear gunfire in the distance and could see trees splintering all around me as bullets riddled their trunks, a testimony to the massive weaponry they were using.

I ran at full speed for about a good ten minutes. I was weighed down by the rifles draped around both shoulders and the duffel bag. Every direction I looked in seemed to be identical. Confused, frustrated, and breathing heavily, I resolved that I had to stand and fight. There was absolutely no way in hell I could get away. I had to waste those jerks, then figure a way out of this woodland maze.

Adrenaline pumped through my body. My will to survive was strong. I had to live. My baby needed me. I would get to see him one day. I might not know him physically by then, but my maternal instincts would come through. But right now, I had to plan. So in the humid weather, I lay down on the ground and frantically covered myself and the duffel bag with leaf litter.

I lay there totally camouflaged. The army green sweatshirt and pants I had on blended in nicely with my surroundings. I was deathly still, breathing in intervals, hoping and praying I didn't have another snake encounter. *This time, I'll be ready for them*, I thought, as I felt the cold steel resting on my stomach. I had some time to think. I didn't know how this was going to turn out. Truthfully, I was struck by a wicked kind of excitement.

I couldn't describe my feelings. I struggled to control my racing thoughts. I recognized that my fragile state of mind was in danger of plunging back into insanity.

The taste I'd never hoped to develop now consumed me. I'd gone through a lake of fire, and now I thirsted for blood—the blood of those who'd caused me so much pain. I lay there, realizing that the training I'd received was kicking in. My instincts were taking over, suppressing my feelings, choking my morals, and killing off any compassion I may have felt. Before this, I would never in a million years have thought about an ambush. But now I was a vicious predator, waiting on my unsuspecting prey to fall helplessly into my trap.

I didn't have too long to wait. From my position, I could see that three of them were approaching. The fools didn't even have the common sense to spread out so that the enemy couldn't easily get the drop on them all at once. My heart thumped savagely with the beat of revenge. And when they were in range, I sat up as though I were *Friday the 13th*'s Jason Voorhees, surprising the shit out of the three would-be assassins.

Quickly, I squeezed the trigger of my assault rifle, spraying deadly rounds through the air, all of which found their marks, turning the men into Swiss cheese. One dropped lifelessly to the ground and another fell to his knees, gripping at the wounds in his chest. The third never stopped coming for me. He'd dropped his weapon when I pumped a couple into him. He was yelling wildly as he approached, but I didn't panic. I calmly let him get a few feet away from me, and then I blew out the back of his head.

I jumped to my feet, sprinting toward the one bent over on his knees, and without thinking, I shot him in the back of his head. I had no sympathy for these jerks. They were there to take my life. But it wasn't for the taking, not today.

I gathered up my belongings quickly. The creeps had dropped a bag. I picked it up and checked it. The thing was filled with C-4 explosives. It would come in handy so I took it. The commotion would draw more attention, and as I hurried away from the carnage, I wondered how many jerks were out there. They were all going to die. So far the number of bastards I'd dusted was four.

My second plan of ambush was spectacular. The men were loud. I couldn't believe they were out in the middle of nowhere, discussing pussy. They walked right past me as I jumped out of a tree and sprayed them bloody. Two more dead. At this point, I was glad that there was no mirror for me to look in. I feared the reflection that would stare back at me. I felt deranged, simply deranged. My hair was a mess. I was a ravenous black woman. I couldn't stop. A fever of insanity ravaged my body. The more bastards that I dusted, the more my appetite for destruction grew.

From my new hiding spot, I could hear the voices of others, two with heavy Italian accents and one who spoke only Italian. This had to be the last of them. I smiled from inside the hollowed log I'd found lying on the ground. It was long enough to support me and my quickly depleting duffel bag of ammunition. Now down to two Glocks, I was no match for the automatics the men possessed. The element of surprise was all I needed to even the score.

I patiently waited until the goons were in my trap before I pushed the button on a silver detonator that resembled a television remote. The explosions were immediate, followed by tortured screaming and cussing. After the commotion died down, I carefully stuck my head out to survey the damage caused by the C-4 explosives. I could see body parts scattered all about, arms, flaming torsos, legs, heads that still held that surprised look in the eyes—just a gruesome, bloody mess.

Some of the trees were still on fire. I didn't care though. I was spent. Now I had to figure a way out. But before I could pull my entire body from the log, I was violently yanked out by my hair. The next thing I felt was the cold steel of a huge hunting blade under my throat.

My captor spoke Italian. Thanks to the time I'd spent listening to Max, I understood him clearly. What I did next surprised him, and me. Seeing the jerk had grabbed me from behind, I took his free hand, bringing it gently to my breasts, indicating to him that I wanted to make love, not war. Sex was an international language. The horny bastard understood; he started breathing heavily, grabbing at my breasts and pussy.

I twisted the knife hand until I possessed the big blade, facing him. Then, before he realized what had hit him, I plunged the Rambo knife dead center into his forehead. I was running before the body dropped.

"*Morte!*" I yelled over my shoulder, running full speed. I expected to be gunned down from behind. But nothing. Night had settled. The only thing I could hear was the wind in my face. I must've run for twenty minutes before I stumbled onto a highway, collapsing. A trucker saw me, picked me up, and drove me to the hospital.

"That's my story," I said calmly into the microphone. I looked up, peeping into the sound room, and saw Kimpa crying. Donna was also in tears, blowing her nose melodramatically into a tissue. I saw Mindsnitch holding back his water. It looked like he was pondering something. Then a look of pure disbelief crossed his face.

"What?" was my only response.

"You ladies have each been through quite an ordeal, but do you really think hijacking this show is gonna help your cause?" he asked smugly.

"Yeah, women have to deal with pigs like you every day. I'm gonna make damn sure that my sistahs stand strong in the face of abuse. And for the record, change your attitude about women or"—I brought the pistol up to his face—"you will be visited again."

Kimpa and Donna walked into the studio.

"I want you to see something," Donna said, pointing. "Look at all the lines lighting up. Those are people calling in with something to say." Donna went to Mindsucka's side. "Let's take some of those calls." Donna went back into the sound room, followed closely by Kimpa—who was still whining about her cramps.

We took a few calls. Every last one was a woman congratulating and saluting us for taking such an extreme approach in promoting women's self-esteem. To my surprise, we hadn't heard from the law again. I reasoned that they'd seen far too many hostage situations go sour.

The private line urgently rang. Mindsnake picked up. He answered a series of questions with "yes" and "no."

"We're on midday news," Kimpa said excitedly, pushing in a twenty-seven-inch color television atop a rolling stand. She plugged it in and turned it on. My eyes nearly bulged from their sockets when I got a gander of the police force surrounding the station. I looked at the clock on the wall. The time had flown past. It hadn't seemed like we'd been in the studio for six hours. It was now twelve noon.

"We're live on location," the reporter said, standing in front of a police barricade with tons of citizens standing behind it, "where two women accosted Mindspeak—a famous radio personality—at six o'clock this morning with weapons and pushed their way into the building. Sources are not yet confirmed but we believe that the report was made by a security officer using his cell phone from somewhere in the building. The police are trying to negotiate with the two women as we speak. It's clear that the two women are using the show's national coverage to tell their horrible tales of abuse perpetrated by ex-boyfriends. And behind us, as you can see"—he pointed behind him at the scores of people waving protest signs of support behind the barricade—"people have shown up in record numbers to support these women. Stay tuned as we will keep you informed and bring you new developments on this breaking story. I'm Luke Chapman, reporting to you live from the city's eastside."

My breath caught in my throat as I observed the enormous crowd of supporters positioned behind the police blockades, squad cars, and armed policemen. The phone rang again. Mindspeak answered, then motioned for one of us. I picked up the phone. A negotiator wasted no time asking me if there were any demands. I informed him that we would give ourselves up on one condition: that we could walk out without the humiliation of handcuffs. He agreed.

A helicopter hovered overhead. I knew the cops would agree. Because of our new, extremely large fan following, the authorities wouldn't dare try anything stupid.

"You women are courageous," Donna said. "At first, I thought you two were demented; some serious head cases." She smiled pleasantly, wiping at her eyes with a tissue. "I'm proud of you girls, real proud." She kissed Kimpa and me on our cheeks.

At that moment, thoughts of the baby I had given birth to but had never seen again crossed my mind. I couldn't believe, nor could I understand, the person I'd become. The new me was very complex. Violent. Respect was paramount.

Kimpa and I shared some similarities but, mostly, we were as different as night and day. Kimpa was me, four years ago; a virgin to firearms. She didn't want the one she was holding, but she was still my sister. In truth, she was a gentle spirit and nothing was wrong with that. Brody had messed her over. The lady had given so much of herself to that bastard. She'd made his career and all he'd given her in return were bruises and a damaged self-esteem. My girl deserved better. She deserved to have her pain eased and her baby returned. I prayed that I could give her the happiness she longed for. I knew a ton of ways to inflict punishment. Any number of them would suit that bastard. I'd give him a homemade vasectomy with a broken pop bottle if I ever ran into the coward.

While Kimpa and Donna were discussing our situation, I stood and straightened out my wrinkled pants, thinking about my first stop after surviving the gun battle with Max's goons in the woods.

I'd gone by my aunt and uncle's, hoping that Denairo was wrong about them being dead. But when I got there, the house was boarded up. I couldn't even produce tears. A neighbor confirmed the horror: they were killed alright; execution-style. Through a friend, I'd found out that Lisa had gotten married to the guy she had been dating when I'd last spoken with her and moved to Orlando.

"Kimpa, you ready to do this?" I asked.

"Yup, let's get this over with."

Hand in hand, we walked out into the lobby with Donna on our heels. Kimpa gave me a devilish grin, nodding at the closet door. "Gonna let 'im out?"

"Let the Hunchback of Notre Dame stay in there." I turned to face her. I looked to the mob outside the window and back to Kimpa. "You ready?"

"Let's do it," she said, smiling. "I'm ready to close this chapter of my life and start anew. All this would make a great story, hunh?"

I smiled, grabbed the 9mm, and laid it on the guard's desktop, along with Roscoe. It pained me to perform such a task. I'd grown quite fond of his nickel-plated ass but I wasn't gonna give the police a reason to shoot me. We faced the door like two award-winning actresses about to take the stage to put on a stunning Broadway play.

"Whatever happens," Kimpa told me, hugging me like I was her favorite teddy bear, "I love you. You'll forever be my sister."

"Yeah. Me, too," was all I could manage. Staying all those years with Denairo had numbed me to sentimental gestures.

"God bless," Donna said, holding up both hands, displaying crossed fingers.

We took deep breaths before I opened the door, saying in unison, "It's show time."

Outside was a circus. We were warmly welcomed by a deafening cheer. I mean, people went nuts at the first sight of us. They yelled our names and held up supportive signs. STOP THE ABUSE read one of them. WE LOVE YOU GIRLS was another. FREE KIMPA AND ISIS declared yet another.

We were major celebrities. The police didn't even see fit to handcuff us. Hell, some of them wore smiles on their faces.

"Hey, stop!" Mindfart yelled, running to catch up to us, almost out of breath.

The police stepped between Mindspitter and us. He looked like he had something weighing heavily on his mind that he needed to discuss before we left. Donna looked confused so she also stepped into the shot of the news camera trained on our little circle.

"I want to press charges on these ladies for kidnapping, unlawful entry of private property, felony firearms, and any damn thing else I could think of," Mindspeak ranted like a crazed lunatic.

"Sir," a light-complexioned officer spoke up, shoving Mind-shitter back, "you'll get a chance to lodge your complaints. Come downtown with us and we'll get you squared away."

"I'm giving you fair warning to get out of our faces," I said. "I've given you fair warning."

"Mindspeak," Donna stepped in, "how could you? These women have been—"

"I don't care what the hell they claim to have been through. People can't take the law into their own hands. And besides, given their attitudes, they probably deserved to be beat—"

Mindstinker wasn't given a chance to finish his thought before Donna hauled off and knocked the purple piss out of him. He dropped to the pavement like he had a ton of bricks resting on his shoulders, and on live television.

"Look out," I said, breaking free of the officer, giving Donna dap and standing over Mindstank. "I gave you a warning," I said, bringing laughter to the surrounding crowd close enough to hear. I gazed determinedly into the television camera. "See that, America, see how he"—I pointed to an unconscious Mindstinker— "crumbled behind the flying female fist of freedom. Women. Are. Not. Inferior."

We left Donna trying to shake the pain from her fist, and Mindspender stretched out on the pavement, the news crew stepping over his unconscious ass to keep the cameras rolling on us. The heifer couldn't convince me that decking her hog of a boss didn't swell her C-cups with pride. I know it didn't leave me feeling the least bit badly. Sometimes, in order to figuratively strike a blow for a cause, you have to literally get physical. Snatch some collars.

Kimpa looked like she was eating up the attention. I had to admit, it did feel refreshing. After all the shit we'd gone through, we deserved this parade-style atmosphere. We saw other news reporters scrambling to get responses in the crowd. A couple of them rushed us for an exclusive. The clowns were stumbling over each other, jockeying for position. Kimpa jumped a little when one of the hounds touched her arm, getting a little too friendly. Being real protective over my sister, I pushed Kimpa behind me, and then I punched the crap out of an overly aggressive reporter. He was all beef and no chin; the reporter hit the pavement like sausages being slapped into a skillet of hot grease. I still had it.

The policeman quickly closed in around us, becoming a protective barrier, shielding us from the media frenzy. They ushered us to a waiting police cruiser. The crowd was going bananas. I couldn't hear a thing.

The closer we came to the vehicles, the louder the crowd roared. I held Kimpa's hand. The cop next to Kimpa was a nice-looking brother—a little short for my taste, but handsome. He kept his eyes on her backside. It didn't take much detective work to figure out that he was sweet on her. Kimpa did have a Rihanna thing jumping off.

In the midst of all the chaos going on, my gut told me that something wasn't right. I hadn't felt like this since the Denairo days. Not since the deadly fight with the hit men. The one thing that my abduction had done for me was sharpen my sense of awareness.

I quickly scanned the crowd, but came up with nothing. That didn't comfort me. Somewhere in the area, the mob lurked. This was what they lived for. With all the media here, this was a chance to show the world that their brand of terror could reach anybody. To murder someone on live television was one way to send the other crime families a powerful message.

My attention focused on the area to my right. The officer on my right shoulder was much different from the officer who was sweatin' Kimpa. The jerk was a tall drink of water. I probably came to his navel. He looked to be Italian born but I wasn't sure.

Out of the corner of my eye, I could see him sizing me up. The punk wore an arrogant smirk. His blond bushy moustache reminded me of a shaggy sheep dog, and when he smiled, it looked like the thing was begging for food.

I could see traces of blond hair sprouting from underneath his police hat.

Although his eyes were covered by a cheap pair of cop glasses, I could tell that he had been sent to kill me. There was no denying it.

It was no surprise when he grabbed me from behind. He had his arm around my throat in a chokehold, but with his free hand, he removed his service automatic from the holster and put it to my head.

When the police found out what was going on, pistols were aimed in our direction. The crowd grew silent, anticipating the worst. But the news hounds kept on rolling footage. I could see this scene splashed across the front page of tomorrow's editions of *The Detroit News* and *The Detroit Free Press.*

The idiot yelled out his demands in a heavy Italian accent. We slowly danced in circles. He didn't want to give the cops a clear shot. With one swipe of the barrel of his gun, he removed his cap and glasses. As the items fell to the hot pavement, I saw that the jerk's eyes were bugging out. He had the chokehold applied so tightly, he was almost cutting off my wind.

"This bitch caused my family lots of problems." He struggled with me, sweating profusely. "This shit stops here. I will show my loyalty."

I quickly came to understand the jerk's situation. I'd heard Max speak about this type of action. If a member of his family committed an act of cowardice, he could redeem himself by perpetrating an act of violence that would redeem him in the eyes of his bosses.

The negotiator, who looked like the spitting image of Richard Roundtree, wore a navy blue police-issued, bulletproof vest. "Remain calm. Nobody has to get hurt here. Just tell us what it is that you want."

My fingers were desperately prying into his hairy forearms, trying to loosen his grip so I could get air into my lungs.

"Bitch!" he shouted at me, foaming at the sides of his mouth, throwing me around like I was a rag doll.

Kimpa looked frantic. He whipped me around again. I could see Donna. Her hands were cupped over her mouth. She was crying and sniffling. I took a minute to size up the situation. I figured that the cops were at a major disadvantage. This jerk was holding a good hand. I wasn't a gambling woman but I'd bet it would be up to me to free myself.

For the better half of a moment, this idiot mumbled something in Italian. Then he spoke English. "Get me"—he looked like the helicopter was irritating him—"I want an unmarked car. And if that copter follows me, I swear, I'll do this bitch!"

What a load of hogwash, I mused. The moron was going to do me anyway. That was his sole purpose.

While he talked, I was sizing up his weaknesses. Although he was gigantic, he still could go down. I could go for the throat, but that would be stupid. I wouldn't have leverage. I'd have to jump up to get to his throat. The nuts were the only other option and they hung almost near my shoulders. Because of his height and size, he was slow.

The big fool mumbled in Italian the whole time we waited on our so-called getaway car. I had other plans. I didn't know who would get the itchy trigger finger first and I wasn't waiting around to see. Even with all the weapons waving around, it surprised me to see the crowd was still in place. Nobody said a word. They stood in stunned silence.

Every step the giant jerk took, his movements were tracked by police weapons.

Somewhere in the crowd, men just like the goon holding me were lurking. Denairo automatically crossed my mind. Was he on top of one of the surrounding buildings with his sights fixed on me? I shuddered. Wherever he was, my baby couldn't be too far behind. I hadn't survived all those years with Denairo only to let this goon take me out. Never! I would see my baby again. Would hold him. Kiss him.

The police finally delivered our chariot. I could see that the boys in blue were absolutely clueless. I was about to raise my heel to drive it into the top of the maggot's foot when his body violently snapped backward like he'd been punched by an invisible fist. His grip slipped.

The crowd must've seen what was going on; everybody fell silent, their eyes filled with horror. And that's when I turned to see the fool falling to the ground with a gaping hole—dead center—in the middle of his forehead. It was like the whole scene was playing in super slow motion. I scanned around, looking for the police who'd put me in the line of fire. I was getting ready to break off some serious violence on the cop with the itchy trigger finger when I discovered that no one on the ground had taken the shot.

The police were scrambling around, trying to figure out where the shot had been fired from, but I was already aware. This body had Denairo's fingerprints all over it. With my right hand shading my eyes, I scanned the rooftops and spotted him on top of a building about a block away. I couldn't see clearly, but it was him. You don't live with a hit man for four years and not recognize his work.

Kimpa ran to me and we hugged like two little girls shivering in a corner during a thunderstorm. I scanned the building again to see if Denairo was still there, but if he had been there, he'd disappeared. In my heart, I cried for the child that I was never going to see again. I grieved because in twenty years, the kid would be conditioned to kill, abandoned of feelings and emotions. I didn't know what was in store for my future, but it could be no worse than my past.

"Them some bad bitches," a heavyset dark-skinned sistah wearing frizzy-looking cornrows said, jumping from her seat, dropping the Detroit newspaper. She'd just finished reading a huge column dedicated to Isis and Kimpa. It'd been almost two months since the incident at the radio station and Isis' and Kimpa's courageous story still dominated the local and national media.

"Can you not use the word 'bitch'? It's so degrading," asked a slender white chick with red hair and deep-set eyes, sitting at a back table with another white woman.

"Sharon," Cornrows said, "don't start with that bullshit, bitch. You know what I mean. Where I'm from, 'bitch' is a term of endearment. But I couldn't possibly ask you to understand nothin' 'bout the hood."

An elderly woman wearing a hairnet, apron, and a nametag with DORIS engraved on it in big black letters worked behind the cafeteria counter.

"Well," Doris said, using a broom to sweep debris into a pile, "I know about your so-called 'hood' because I'm from the projects, but I still don't like that word."

"Amen, Doris," said a woman sitting by herself, holding a black leather Bible.

Cornrows sat back down with a frustrated look on her face.

"Do you think Isis and Kimpa went through hell to make great strides for us women only to have you dishonor their sacrifices by continuing to set women back using your so-called 'term of endearment'?" Doris preached, never breaking stride in her sweeping. "That's blasphemy around here. You're sitting in the seat that they once sat in. You're living in the shelter that they lived in. That's why the owner of this place felt compelled to rename it the *Kimpa and Isis Mission*."

Even though Doris was revered and regarded as grandmomma by the abused and neglected women in the shelter, the old lady wasn't shy about offering her opinion.

"Kimpa is on *Oprah*." A short, light-skinned woman wearing a T-shirt bearing the images of Isis and Kimpa with the words WOMAN + STRENGTH = RESPECT captioned underneath rushed in and turned on the television positioned in the corner of the cafeteria.

The women in the cafeteria settled in to watch the show. Kimpa looked fabulous, sitting right next to Oprah and glowing radiantly.

*"So what's life been like for Kimpa Peoples these past two months?" Oprah asked with a beautiful smile on her face.*

*Kimpa smiled warmly, hesitantly, like she was conjuring up the devils of her past.*

*"Well, Oprah, let me thank you for setting the standard for women across the nation, across the planet. I'm truly honored to be in your presence. But to answer your question, it's been a whirlwind of press, travel, photos, and benefit dinners. I wouldn't have thought that my pain would be so well-received. I'm truly blessed. I could've been dead. But God saw fit to make me one of the ambassadors for the unity of women."*

*Oprah's audience applauded loudly.*

*"Very well put. What's this I hear about a book deal?"*

*"Well, Oprah, yes, I do have a deal with Creative Property publishing company for three books."*

*"We were talking in the green room and I know you wish to exercise humility but I must say this: Kimpa, you also have a movie deal about the ordeal you and Isis went through."*

*"Yes," Kimpa smiled coyly, "Seuss films is set to begin production after the first of the year."*

*"Kimpa, you have to be excited. Girl, before we go to break, I'd be remiss if I didn't ask you about Isis. Where is girlfriend and how is she handling her celebrity?"*

*"Well, Oprah, all I can say is that my sister has been placed in the witness protection program. I haven't had any communication with her and it's hard because we've been through so much together. So, Isis, if you're listening out there, I love you with all my heart."* Kimpa's tears were clearly visible sliding down her face. She'd been through the storm and never imagined that she could've gotten this far without Isis.

*"Before we go to commercial, I would like to bring out the love of your life,"* Oprah said as one of the television crew members brought out Brody Jr. and placed the baby in Kimpa's lap.

*"You want to tell the audience who this little guy is?"*

Kimpa kissed her twelve-month-old infant on his curly head.

*"This is my little man, Brody Jr. Oprah, I have full custody over him."*

*"What about the father?"*

*"All I'm going to say is God don't like ugly. Once the story came out, his publisher pulled his books from stores and he's serving time in a federal penitentiary for tax evasion."*

Oprah looked into the camera and pointed. *"Let that be a lesson, people; pay your taxes. Keep it right here; we'll be right back."*

An hour later, the women at the Isis and Kimpa Mission were having dinner and discussing the *Oprah* show.

"Didn't Kimpa look good, ya'll?" said a shapely, brown-skinned lady with a huge scar running down her forehead, while stuffing her mouth with chicken.

"Yep," Doris said, serving up a plate, "I'm so proud of her. She has a writing career, sole custody of her son, and peace of mind." Doris picked up a glass and lightly tapped on the side with a fork to gain attention. "Listen up. I want everybody in this room to pick up your glass. Let's toast to Isis and Kimpa for giving a lot of us the courage to tackle life one day at a time."

"Hear, hear," the cafeteria spoke in unison, lifting their glasses. "Here's to the queens of unity."

# ABOUT THE AUTHOR

Thomas Slater is a native of Detroit, MI. In '97 he picked
up a pen and scribbled for three months, producing his debut
title *Run with the Pack*, an urban crime thriller. Fed up with the
lack of attention street literature was receiving at the time,
Thomas switched genre-gears in 2004. Drawing on his vast
experience as an assembly worker at American Axle
Manufacturing plant, he fictionalized the chaos and corruptible
plight of the blue-collar worker in his second self-published
venture, *Blue-Collar Diary: Factory Folk Drama*.
His next title, *No More Time-Outs*, will be published in 2011.
Thomas Slater hopes to create a footprint by stepping
off into the cement of literary greatness.
Visit the author at www.hypnoticliterature.com and
facebook.com/thomasslater and email him
at thomaseslater@yahoo.com.

# AUTHOR'S NOTE

There was a time where one literary door slammed in my face after another, rejection letters—I had enough to wallpaper my house, and the neighbors'. Thirteen years of agents and editors from those *agents guides* all giving the same spiel in the form of a very informal desert-dry, mechanically voiced "Dear Author" rejection letter. I was so frustrated and discouraged I stopped writing for an entire year. My pity-parties were extravagant, cabaret status. I almost gave up on my dreams, came awfully close—twice. Then I thought about it: what if all those who had history-impacting dreams simply gave up.

Life would've been totally devoid of prominent inventions and powerful historical-changing figures. If those highly gifted engineers who designed the first printing press in China around 593 A.D. would've shelved the dream of printing—which would've severely had a *trickle-down effect*—there would be no newspapers or slavery abolitionists circulating "free the slave" leaflets. I'm sure that Frederick Douglass's autobiographical *Narrative of the Life of Frederick Douglass* wouldn't exist either—at least not in print—which is regarded to be one of the most influential pieces of literature to fuel the abolitionist movements of the nineteenth century. If giving up would've been optional for the esteem and brilliant W.E.B. DuBois—along with others—he would've become easily discouraged by radical opposition and forsaken the vision for The National Association for the Advancement of Colored People known as the NAACP. Abandoned would be such dreams for a very prestigious all-black institution promoting higher learn-ing called Morehouse College which produced the great Reverend Dr. Martin Luther King, Jr. And of course you know that if he would've forsaken his DREAM—well, I'm sure you get the picture.

When I stopped to think about all those who struggled before me, some in the face of extreme prejudice, I had to go on. I just couldn't discard my dreams. My struggles and perseverance paid handsomely in Zane recognizing my gift. It might've taken me thirteen years, but I'm here finally! Whatever it is you're trying to accomplish, stay the course and believe in God who believes in you!

Thank you, Zane, for all that you've done to promote the vision of others! You're a true gate-keeper of dreams!

—Thomas Slater

# READER'S DISCUSSION GUIDE

1. Besides Isis' ordeal, what was the key element that really drove Isis over the edge and pushed her into formulating a plot to highjack the radio station?

2. Kimpa told Brody that she'd never sold her body before. Was this the truth? And if so, why did she stop?

3. When Kimpa found out that Brody had herpes, do you think she handled the situation correctly?

4. Some believe that people will do anything for fame and fortune; do you think chasing bling blinded Brody to the deadly consequences of breaking his promise with Mafia Incorporate by passing their dirty laundry off as fiction?

5. Three months into Kimpa's second pregnancy, she hid the baby from Brody. Why?

6. What role did Kimpa's best friend and mentor, Sensation, play in Kimpa losing custody of her baby?

7. What excuse did Isis give for ending up on the rooftop with Denairo?

8. Why did Denairo kill Isis' friend, Tisha?

9. What were Isis' feelings toward the hit on 187?

10. When asked about her imprisonment, Denairo kept answering, "You belong to us." What was the true motive behind Isis' kidnapping?

11. It's said that nothing brings people closer than a crisis. When the dust finally settled on their campaign for justice, what was the bond like between Kimpa and Isis?

12. In your estimation, what impact did Kimpa and Isis' efforts to be heard have on the listening world? And how far would you go to seek justice?

STAY TUNED! IF YOU ENJOYED "SHOW STOPPAH,"
BE SURE TO CHECK OUT

# NO MORE TIME-OUTS

BY THOMAS SLATER
COMING FROM STREBOR BOOKS IN FALL 2011

## TEMPEST

Two hours ago I was studying my Bible, reading from the gospel of *Matthew*. What stuck in my mind was committing adultery. My thing was: why make men look so damn attractive? Why is it so hard to follow God's rules? Why make all this stuff appealing to the flesh, and then say, we are not allowed to even think about touching. The more I read the Bible; the more I became confused. This law telling me I risk a permanent vacation in Hell if I commit this sin, or my soul was going to burn for eternity if I didn't repent. How could I stop my mind from wondering about the appetites of the flesh?

It was a good thing God wasn't in the back of my Escalade because Robert was doing all those little things to me the Bible warned as sinful. My father always said evil lurked around using the cover of darkness, covering up the naughtiness of mankind. We were far away from the city, and even farther from my husband. My truck sat in one of the metro parks. I was too drunk to know which one I'd driven to. At this point, while Robert was sinking his love deeper and deeper into me, it really didn't matter. Nothing mattered. Yes, I was married, but Robert was my boy-toy. My maintenance man of choice. I hated sounding clichés, but I was pushed into this affair. My husband was a good man. He was good to me. But he couldn't satisfy me in the bedroom. He'd come along at a time when my self-esteem had been damaged by this bastard of an ex-boyfriend. My husband was cute. Had money. I was lonely. And that's all it took for me to walk down the aisle. I tried for the first year to be a good wife, but when I met Robert that was it. He had power, passion.

"Tempest Jones, Tempest Jones, damn Mrs. Jones," Robert passionately let me know that he was appreciating every inch of my womanhood. "Me and Mrs.—Mrs. Jones…Mrs. Jones, Mrs. Jones."

Robert was an attorney from a very prestigious law firm. The man was a sexual beast, too. He knew my body better than I knew it. Plus, the very long thang swinging between his legs had sealed the deal. My husband and I owned a huge beauty shop, two apartment buildings and a cluster of single homes.

We were going at it pretty hot and heavy now. The windows were fogged up and I was trying hard to keep from screaming while he was pleasuring me like no man had ever done. My ass was facing him while I straddled his lap. I tried desperately to keep my wits about me so that we wouldn't find ourselves crept up on by the park rangers. Robert had the task of watching the back and side windows. No matter how hard we tried to keep watch, our lust blinded us as we slipped deeper into erotic bliss. At the height of my climax I totally let me guard down. No longer was I watching for the law. Hell, we had a good spot anyway. The truck sat in a deserted parking lot a mile off the main road, surrounded by big evergreen trees.

The one thing I did like about having affairs with other men was that they didn't want to cuddle afterward. There was no time to. Really no time for words. Sometimes we did *it*, and said nothing to each other afterward. Just a kiss and a smile and we'd go our own separate ways. And that's what we did. I drove him back to his truck, we kissed and then he went his way, leaving me to go mine.

The night was still young. It was around 11:00 p.m. and I was still very much hungry for flesh. I wondered about Darrius. But that was it. I knew he was probably slaving over paperwork as usual—not giving a damn about me. I wanted to go home but my appetite wouldn't let me. I had just dined on a corporate power lunch. And for my main meal—a young tasty thug. Within one hour I'd managed to go from Cristal to Old English, from a thousand-dollar suit to a saggy pants, Timberland boot-wearing, gun-toting, rough house-walking, rap music-blasting, cold-blooded gangster.

I blamed two people for my open legs condition: r̶ ̶
Reverend Poppa Jones. In her day, my mother had one
She had all the sexual equipment to leave a man lick
wanting to pay for a sample. Moms had average-sized [
with absolutely no assistance from a good bra—the girls always stood
at attention. Her delectable swell blended in nicely with her narrow
waistline. And just when roaming eyes thought it was over, her flawless
waistline tapered downward and ballooned into a beautiful, well-
proportioned back-side. Her legs held muscular definition. My ol' girl
used to be strapped. And that's the body I was tramping around town
in now. I'd inherited my Mom's whole package.

Unlike my mother, though, I was out of control with my hourglass
figure. I felt God had given me a hot sports car without the owner's
manual. I was an ebony dimepiece in search of a ninety-cent thug so
we could share a whole dollars' worth of good times. Men often told
me that my body was a cross between JLo's and Beyonce's.

I'd been a preacher's kid growing up. That meant we didn't get to
experiment with the world like other kids. We were in church more
than we were at home. I hated every minute of it, too. Back when my
father was the pastor at a small storefront church, times were terrible.
The inside of the church was raggedy, and even when he wasn't
working at Global Engines and Axles manufacturing plant, the good
Reverend spent the rest of his time making repairs to that dump. In
my mind's eyes, kids shouldn't be deprived of life's experiences. They
only end up like me.

It took me forty minutes to get from the suburbs to the 'hood. I
guess I should have been pretty scared driving around the ghetto in
this expensive truck at this time of night. The street looked like a
cemetery: a few burned-down homes and every other house had a
vacant lot next to it. Darkness shared the street with gloom. A few of
the streetlights looked to have been shot out. But that didn't stop me
from observing two vehicles that sat one behind the other, stripped to
the frame.

After I got past the first block the street burst with life. The hustlers
were hustling, the crackheads were stealing, and people walked the
streets searching for whatever people searched for at this time of night.
Another reason I wasn't scared was that my little twenty-year-old thug
ran this part of town. It seemed to be an area that the law had forgotten
about. I'd been coming over here for almost a year now and I had
never seen a police car. This area was rough. It seemed like somebody
was getting blasted every other night. But I had my little thug to protect

.e. Geechie might've been a shrimp of a man, but it was his sinister heart that people feared. He was a dark-skinned brother with pearly white teeth, deep dimples and brushed-wavy hair. His small frame ripped right by mountain ranges of muscle; plus he carried one of those Glock pistols and didn't give a damn about using it. His mouth was foul, but I loved his thuggish drawers.

After I found the house, I pulled up around back. Geechie's company was parked in the alley. As I drove up my headlights flooded the alley, sending big furry rats scattering for cover. This was the part I hated. No sooner than I was out of the truck a strong piss smell struck me in the face. The humidity had the alley smelling like pure hell. I looked around. Nothing but darkness stared back after the timer on my truck headlights disengaged. I expected somebody to jump from the shadows and drag me in to do God knows what. That thought caused me to pull and tug at my short dress.

Walking through flickering backyard lights reminded me that I was still wearing my four-carat diamond ring. The dog barking in the distance caused me to walk a little faster. In the backyard I could smell something that I was praying not to step in. I hadn't paid much attention to the rap music blaring from the house. The security that I received from the private fences surrounding the whole backyard made me feel a little comfortable—not to mention the pair of roguish eyes peering out from one of the top bedroom windows. He yelled something as I switched onto the back porch. The house was kept up immaculately. They even had the nerve to have a flower garden in the front yard. It looked like Suzy Homemaker lived there. But that was a facade. Its real intentions were much more evil.

I was fidgeting with my alarm keypad when the big heavy steel door swung open—followed by the smoke and the strong, skunk smell of marijuana.

"Tell Geechie," the cornrowed-head punk announced as he stared at my body as though I had no clothes on, "that his piece is here." He had a forty-ounce of something in his hand. The worm disgustedly licked his big pink lips and stepped aside to let me in.

I went in through the kitchen, stepping right into a sea of sagging-pants gangsters. Almost everybody and their momma were sporting afros and cornrows like they where staging a *Save the Seventies* rally. For a minute I thought I had stepped onto the set of a gangster rap video. There were a few young women on the scene. None of the little skanks had nothing on me though.

Once I entered all eyes were wall-papered to me. My mouthwatering cleavage reminded me that at age thirty-five I was still the hottest bitch at the party. A gorgeous Dolce and Gabbana dress covered my body, yielding about mid thigh. Manolo Blahnik shoes, Hublot watch—three carats of course—and a Gucci handbag that cost more than all the outfits and nappy hair weaves that these little hood rats were sporting combined—completed my ensemble. They stared in hot envy—even though they probably didn't know about half the designers I had on.

The rap music was unbearably loud. Unlike the outside of the house, the inside looked like a trash bin. Beer bottles, cigarette butts, pizza boxes and burger wrappers littered the floors.

I put a real sensual twist in my hips to give those tramps something really to look at. I stepped into the living room and I saw where everybody was. I said *hi* to everybody I knew. There were two couples dancing—grinding I should say. A dice game had just broken out in a corner of the dining room. And a whole cluster of thugs were chillin' out on the couch and love seat drinking, smoking and talking about some guy that they'd shot up. The guy wearing a huge, uneven nappy afro was even acting out the shooting incident. A den of thieves. I had ventured into a den of thieves. I almost choked to death on all the smoke.

"Ay, homie, ain't that that ol' broad who run the beauty shop on Grand River?" I heard one of the guys mention to the other.

*Old broad*, I thought. You know I was smoking. *Pissed* and *disrespected* for better words.

"Yeah, man, I dropped my bitch off at that joint a few times. Not bad for an ol' broad," his baldheaded boy responded.

I almost said something to them. And when I was about to go ghetto, Flash, Geechie's right-hand man, walked up.

"Yo, Geechie waitin' on you upstairs." He noticed the uneasy look on my face. "What's ya problem?"

"Just a little disrespect down here!"

"Which one?"

I nodded my head in the direction of a big light-skinned guy wearing a bald head and one of those long hairy goatees. The guy was big but Flash was enormous. Flash was a black hole color with huge hands and feet. He had a T-Rex-like neck. Without words, Flash stomped right up to the guy, whirled him around in my direction, and then warned if I was ever disrespected again, he would make sure that he'd be gumming grapes. Flash slapped the guy upside his head with an open hand and shoved him in my direction. Nobody said anything; they got out of the way to make room for the beat down. The guy walked up to me with a petrified look on his face. He apologized a few times. Flash snarled at the rest of the baggy pants—hip-hoppers—and then escorted me upstairs to an empty bedroom.

"Geechie handlin' some bidness. So chill. He'll be up in a sec." I did what he said. I walked into the room and took a seat on an older wicker chair. I thought against sitting on the bed; didn't know what kind of germs lived on sheets. Flashed closed the door leaving me alone to deal with my conscience. Flash was scary. There were rumors circulating about him working as a contract killer. And judging from the respect that was given downstairs, it only confirmed his deadly job.

I sat there fighting good, trying to rationalize the evil that I was getting into. I had a nice business, a nice husband and all the love in the world. Any other woman would have been happy, but not me. I tried not to think of my mother's condition. Didn't want it to ruin my mood. I was developing a small headache from the strong smoke and the alcohol that I had consumed earlier.

Twenty minutes later, Geechie strolled in. He didn't even offer an apology for holding me that long. His beady little eyes devoured my figure. I could see an erection bulging from his baggy jeans. He offered a toothy grin, almost sinister-like. I was violently grabbed. I liked it. Without words, he threw me harshly onto the nasty sheets. Before I could object he had my dress up, panties down and working it like a young gangster was supposed to. I was having a good time but somehow I knew that God would have the last laugh. If you lie down with dogs, you get up with fleas. I didn't know what I had gotten myself into. All I knew was that every good right came to an even faster stop. I was down...dirty and awaiting judgment.

It was almost three in the morning and the party downstairs showed no sign of letting up. 50 Cent's vocals were crystal clear and the bass was vibrating underneath my bare feet. It seemed as if I was standing right on top of a speaker. I don't know which one I hated more: how I felt after my sexual appetite had been fulfilled or washing up in this nasty bathroom that resembled a trucker's rest stop. The toilet seat was down and piss stained it like a portrait of urine-sanity. The tile on the bathroom floor was filthy. And the little light that the sixty-watt light bulb cast revealed a God-awful, deep dark ring around the bathtub. The sink in which I was bathing was turning black, highlighted by rust stains.

Geechie entered without the courtesy of a knock.

"Yo, ma," Geechie said. He never smiled. I guess ruthless men like him had no time to smile. "I need to go to the dealership but I ain't got no credit. I need you to put a ride in yo' name for me."

I might've been whipped by this young buck, but I wasn't stupid. I knew the risk of such an action. If he had been caught by the police on drug possession, the repercussion would be devastating to my business and family.

"I don't think I could—"

Geechie violently grabbed me by the throat. He shook me so hard my naked breast painfully slapped against my arms.

With clenched teeth, he said, "You will do what the hell I say do." He released me. As my naked body dropped to the floor I grabbed for my throat and inhaled deeply. "Do we understand each other?" I said nothing as I continued to struggle for air. He bent at the waist and grabbed a handful of my hair. "I said...do we understand each other?"

"Okay," was all I could manage. I'd brought this all on myself. I had to oblige. I knew if I didn't, there was no telling what Geechie would do.

He looked at me with an evil grin. "Now if you be a good little girl, I might...just...might let you ride in my new 'Vette." A more malicious grin ripped across his chin. "Get dressed and get out."

On my drive home I checked the messages on my cell phone. There was one message from Wisdom and one message from Momma, but I couldn't understand why there were no messages from Darrius. I drove at break-necking speed trying to flee from the ghetto. I was on the freeway now thinking about my life, Momma's illness and how I hated Yazoo's guts. I don't know if I hated him for adding to Momma's stress or I hated him for really knowing the truth about my trampish ways. I had no kids. I was only responsible for myself. Thank God I had no little girls. I didn't have the morals of an alley cat, so I definitely wouldn't have been able to teach her a thing about life.

Silently, I drove toward Bloomfield Hills Township. A right and two lefts and another right put me into the drive of my fabulous column-style home. I hit the button of the garage door opener and as I watched the door ascend, I thought about Geechie. During the first part of our little affair, he had been well behaved. I knew he was violent but up until now, he had never showed any aggression toward me. I figured he thought that he had this old lady hooked. And now he was able to use me at his calling. The undying truth *was* that I was hooked. I needed that thug in my life. I needed the lawyer, too. The horror was that I needed a different man to fit all of my desires.

I pulled in right alongside my husband's 600 series Benz, thinking of an excuse that I could give for being so late. I walked into the kitchen through the garage entry, removing my heels. This part of the house accommodated stainless steel appliances complete with a nice size marble island. I walked through the kitchen, my bare feet slapping against the marble floor and up our spiral staircase right into the master bedroom. Darrius was a covered-up lump in our California King. He didn't move. He didn't do anything. I cut on the lights to get some response. He sluggishly stirred but never awoke. I wanted him to wake up and hold me. Kiss me. But instead, all I heard was snoring. I threw a silent hissy fit on my way to the bathroom, closed the door, and turned the shower on as hot as I could bear. I sat on the toilet watching the steam rise and still thinking about all my skeletons. I sat for a moment before I shed my clothes. I glanced at my naked body through the steam-filmed mirror, hating the whore that stared back. I started crying as I jumped into the shower, trying like hell to scrub all my sins away.